温州大学中文学科建设丛书

幻想

曼斯菲尔德短篇小说论

The Treatment of Fantasy in Katherine Mansfield's Short Stories

英汉对照

张　翎◎著

陈　彦◎中文译者

张　翎◎译文修订

ZHEJIANG UNIVERSITY PRESS

浙江大学出版社

·杭州·

图书在版编目（CIP）数据

幻想：曼斯菲尔德短篇小说论：英汉对照 / 张翎
著. -- 杭州：浙江大学出版社，2023.3
ISBN 978-7-308-23510-5

Ⅰ. ①幻… Ⅱ. ①张… Ⅲ. ①曼斯菲尔德
(Mansfield, Katherine 1888-1923)－小说研究－英、汉
Ⅳ. ①I561.074

中国国家版本馆CIP数据核字(2023)第020423号

幻想：曼斯菲尔德短篇小说论：英汉对照

张翎　著

责任编辑	牟琳琳
责任校对	吕倩岚
责任印制	范洪法
封面设计	尤含悦
出版发行	浙江大学出版社
	（杭州市天目山路148号　　邮政编码　310007）
	（网址：http://www.zjupress.com）
排　　版	杭州林智广告有限公司
印　　刷	杭州宏雅印刷有限公司
开　　本	710mm×1000mm　1/16
印　　张	10.75
字　　数	152千
版 印 次	2023年3月第1版　2023年3月第1次印刷
书　　号	ISBN 978-7-308-23510-5
定　　价	79.00元

作者　张　翎

　　海外华文作家。代表作有《劳燕》《余震》《金山》等。小说获华语传媒年度小说家奖，华侨华人文学奖评委会大奖，《中国时报》开卷好书奖，红楼梦奖（世界华文长篇小说奖）专家推荐奖等文学奖项。根据其小说《余震》改编的影片《唐山大地震》，获得亚太影展最佳影片和大众电影百花奖最佳影片奖。小说被译成多国语言。

译者　陈　彦

　　比较文学博士，暨南大学外国语学院教师。

曼斯菲尔德肖像，摄于1914年。
由新西兰惠灵顿亚历山大·特恩布尔图书馆提供

温州大学中文学科建设丛书
总序

孙良好

　　温州大学中国语言文学学科的历史文脉可以追溯到晚清学术大师、教育家孙诒让先生于1906年创建的温州师范学堂。在百年的历史积淀中，一代词宗夏承焘、戏曲宗匠王季思、经史学家周予同、古文字学家戴家祥、著名作家王西彦、敦煌学专家蒋礼鸿、戏曲学家徐朔方、九叶诗人唐湜等先贤曾在此求学或执教，为本学科铸就了深厚的人文底蕴。

　　斯文不坠，薪火相传。

　　进入21世纪以来，本学科广纳天下英才，发展态势喜人。2003年，文艺学、汉语言文字学两个二级学科及相关的民俗学获批硕士学位授权点。2010年，获批一级学科硕士学位授权点。2016年，成为浙江省"十三五"一流学科A类。2017年，学科下属"浙江传统戏曲研究与传承中心"成为浙江省哲学社会科学重点研究A类基地。2019年，与本学科紧密关联的汉语言文学专业成为首批国家级一流本科专业建设点。

　　目前，本学科已形成中国古代文学、中国古典文献学、文艺学、中国现当代文学、汉语言文字学等5个优势学科方向，戏曲研究、域外汉文献研究、文艺美学研究、汉藏语言比较研究、鲁迅研究、温州文学与文化研究等在海内外学界颇具影响力。其中，以南戏研究为龙头的传统戏曲研究，有力地支持了浙南区域文化建设；域外汉文献和东亚俗文学的对接研究以及汉藏语言比较研究，可以为"一带一路"的文化交流提供重要支撑；以文艺学为基础的审美文化研究，注重理论与实践的结合，拓展出语言诗学、神话美学、地域文学、媒介传播等特色方向。

回首来时路，瞻望未来梦。我们编纂本丛书，旨在集中推出一批高水平的学术成果，或继往开来，或引领潮流，或特色鲜明，打造温州大学中文学科品牌，续写新的历史篇章。

关于曼斯菲尔德的一些杂想

（代序）

　　最初知道这位作家，是从徐志摩的一篇悼念文章里，他管她叫曼殊菲儿。曼殊菲儿这个名字和徐志摩文中"仙姿灵态"的形象很是契合。在他笔下，她从衣饰妆容、言语做派，以及病恹恹的身子骨上都有些接近林黛玉。后来在别的地方再次遇见她，她就不叫这个名字了。假若徐志摩在天有灵，知道他如此仰慕的曼殊菲儿已经被规范成了曼斯菲尔德，就如同他的翡冷翠已经变为佛罗伦萨的时候，不知该作何想？窃以为：人文地理的外国名字，终究还是诗人翻译得传神。

　　用今天的话来说，徐志摩面对这位奇女子时，很有几分小迷弟般的战战兢兢。因了私底里的仰慕，他对曼殊菲儿在文学上的评价，就不免带了些主观的情愫。比如他说"她已经在英国的文学界里占了一个很稳固的位置"，这话倒也未必。从彼时到今日，在英语文学世界的大部分人眼中，曼斯菲尔德（虽不情愿，我还是使用规范化的译名吧）一直都处于较为边缘的位置。我在复旦大学外文系读英美文学本科的时候，似乎不曾从任何一门课的老师嘴里听说过这个名字。当然，那时的课程设计有相当一部分的内容是放置在外语技能上的，文学课是某种意义上粗框大条的"科普"，只能挑最重要的作家来做一遍按年代的梳理而已。后来我到加拿大卡尔加里大学读英语文学研究生，课程就分得细致了，细到我惶然不知所措的地步：按年代，按地域，按文体，按流派……可是她的名字依旧难得一见。我是在"维多利亚时期女性主义作家"和"英联邦国家作家"这两个小圆圈的狭窄重合处，偶然找到了关于她的一些介绍。

　　我把她选为我毕业论文的研究对象，最初的起因当然是徐志摩。但徐志摩只是把我引到了门口，真正让我决定跨入门里的，还是因为一己私心——

我想找一条不那么拥挤的路走。我总不至于选莎士比亚吧？可怜的莎翁，身上的每一个毛孔都已经被高倍放大镜细细探察过了，连他十四行诗中那个神秘的"黑肤女郎"，都已经成为无数篇论文的考证对象。我还能翻出什么新花样？基于同样的原因，我也不会选择诸如狄更斯、哈代、伍尔芙之类的名流。曼斯菲尔德一生的作品，不过三五个短篇小说集子，关注她的人群，也相对稀少。我稍加努力，总能找到一两个新鲜的缺口。

从这个搬不上台面的动机出发，我开始认真研读她的作品。在她的字里行间，我找到了一些独立于徐志摩印象之外的感觉。与徐志摩笔下那个面泛潮红、带着肺气声说话的病弱女子相比，书里的那个声音则呈现了长着钩角的尖刻和凌厉。她的情绪强烈，很少能找到圆融的余地。她小说里的女主人公们憎恶婚姻，憎恶婚姻里丈夫对性无止境的索取，憎恶女性沦为生育机器、为养育儿女维持家务所陷入的平庸生活，憎恶体面社会的伪善和社交规范的繁文缛节……这些女性主义的觉醒意识，在其他维多利亚时期的女作家（如伍尔芙）的作品里也有非凡的表述，并未让我格外诧异。最震撼我的，反倒是她对底层生活状态的同情和对贫富不均的社会现象的反映。她在《帕克大妈》里对那位贫穷孤苦的老女佣、《园会》中对那位意外身亡的年轻车夫的描述，让我在恍惚之间依稀看到了高尔基和柔石的影子。

曼斯菲尔德出生于新西兰的一个显赫家族，祖父是国会议员，父亲是新西兰著名的银行家并被授予爵位。她在优渥的家境中长大，被父亲送往英伦接受教育，后来就一直在欧洲生活。成年后虽然也有为钱袋担忧的时候，但那种担忧仅限于租什么样的房子、度多久的假之类的事务，她从来不曾真正沦落到捉襟见肘的地步。她对贫富分化的愤怒，更多源于她对社会现状的关注。

曼斯菲尔德二十九岁染上肺结核——在她的年代，那几乎是绝症。此后她就常年在发烧和咳血之间的短暂间歇中辛苦捱日，未及三十五岁便与世长辞。徐志摩和她度过的那"不死的二十分时间"，已是她一生的最后时光。当时他和她都没有意识到：那是一场延长了数月的回光返照。在病榻上经历的孤独、深知死之将至的恐惧和绝望、对理想和现实之间不可逾越的鸿沟的清醒认知，促使她在小说中反反复复创造了许多 fantasy 场景。fantasy 一词在英语中有着丰富的内涵，把这样一个千层饼一样的词移植到另外一种语言的土壤里，往往只能挑选其中一个层次的含义——这也是历代文学翻译必然面临的挑战。在这个文本中我们把 fantasy 译为"幻想"，也只是一种经过了许多权衡和妥协之后的近义诠释。

回到先前的话题。带着各种阅读印象，我开始动笔书写以曼斯菲尔德小说为主题的毕业论文。我从人物塑造、意象使用、情节推进、结构布局等方面探讨了幻想元素在她小说中所起的作用。这篇论文让我获得了英语文学的硕士学位，但我最终没在学术之路上继续行走下去，而是经过千回百转之后成了小说家。在漫长的谋生和追求写作梦想的旅途中，我和曼斯菲尔德渐行渐远。然而她从未彻底消失，偶尔还会在夜深人静的时刻毫无预兆地闯入我的意识。后来我跟随冯小刚导演为电影《唐山大地震》和《只有云知道》踩点，两度去过曼斯菲尔德出生和度过童年的惠灵顿城。每一次踏上那片土地，曼斯菲尔德的形象就会从岁月的积尘中格外清晰地浮现出来。

几年前我被温州大学聘为驻校作家，有一次和温大人文学院的孙良好院长偶然聊起想把这篇论文译成中文，这一想法得到他极为迅速而积极的回应。于是，经过漫长的修订完善和翻译校对过程之后，这篇论文终于以中英文对照的形式出版——也算是了却了我多年的一个念想。

也许是巧合，这本书上市时，正值曼斯菲尔德辞世 100 周年之际。一个世纪过去了，在她身后，世界又发生了一次大战，无数次小战，有过了广岛长崎，有过了切尔诺贝利，有过了"9·11"；敌人和盟友之间的界限，经历了多次变迁；文学家对月亮星球和宇宙的许多想象，也经由现代科技变为可以部分抵达的现实。徐志摩那篇情真意切的追忆文章里为曼斯菲尔德留下的那道灵光，如今却已经渐渐被人淡忘。阅读和关注她小说的人，越发寥落无几。希望这本书能成为一根火柴，点亮哪怕是一根细细的灯芯，好让路人知道：去往曼斯菲尔德的路未绝，前面或有通幽之处。

感谢温州大学人文学院以及孙良好院长对这个项目的大力支持。也感谢暨南大学文学院前院长王列耀教授的热心引荐，使得我有机会认识暨南大学外国语学院的陈彦老师。陈彦老师在百忙之中应承了这桩费时费事的苦差事，在艰难晦涩的语言和概念转换中辛苦穿行，完成了翻译。"抛砖引玉"是个用得过于烂熟的成语，但我一时找不到一个可以替代的词，就权且留用——期待这篇论文能推开一扇小窗，让汉语世界更多的读者和学者，对曼斯菲尔德的生平和创作产生好奇。

张翎

2022 年 8 月 6 日于多伦多

目　录
CONTENTS

英文部分

中文部分

英文部分

ABSTRACT

One of the under-explored areas in Katherine Mansfield's fictional art is the recurrent use of fantasy. Herbert Gold defines this term as "the dreaming about alternatives which makes men human" (450), while Nadine Gordimer regards it as "a shift in angle" and "a wider lens on ultimate reality" (459–60). Kathryn Hume perceives it more inclusively as "**any departure from consensus reality**, … manifested in innumerable variations, from monster to metaphor" (21). Mansfield herself attributes fantasy to the artist's desire "to create his own world in this world" (*Journal* 273). Three major facts in her life explain her tendency to turn within—her feeling as an outsider ostracized by London literary society, the constant vacillation between a marriage and a lesbian sisterhood, and the impact of the World War I.

Fantasy in her stories functions, first of all, to strengthen the characterization. As she simultaneously believes in and doubts the existence of a unified self, her characters are torn between their indulgence in role-playing and their desire to realize a "true" self. As their subjective vision constantly intrudes onto the objective reality, fantasy becomes a part of characterization. The portrayal of their manifold experiences offers the reader multiple perspectives to probe their psychological depths.

Mansfield has repeatedly expressed her preference for a revelation of soul through suggestive gestures. Her world of fantasy is composed of a series of images rich in associative meanings. While her early works mainly center on "dream figures," her later stories shift the focus to the natural world for figurative expression. In presenting such images and symbols in the realm of fantasy, Mansfield unfolds another controversial aspect of life: an unquenchable desire for truth and love mingled with a despair over the unattainability of them.

Fantasy is also partially responsible for both the departure from and adherence to tradition in her narrative structure. It has three major structural functions—additive, subtractive and contrastive according to Hume's analysis (83). It reinforces the progression of plot and heightens the effect of thematic conflict by revealing the discrepancy between the imagined version of life and the world of reality. The point of recognition is reached when the two come to an open confrontation. Resolution is usually expressed in the moment of perception following the climatic clash.

In most of her stories, fantasy achieves the intended goal of exploring and commenting on the nature of reality. Two basic features of fantasy—the sincerity in her characters' pursuit of truth and love, and their indignation against the brutality of existence—help to establish her as one of the serious writers of the twentieth century.

CHAPTER I

INTRODUCTION: MANSFIELD AND FANTASY

Katherine Mansfield has often been unfairly considered a marginal writer because of insufficient exploration of certain areas in her art. One of these under-explored areas is her use of fantasy, a feature characterizing almost all her stories, from her shy juvenilia to the more mature works composed before her death in 1923. Both her cultists and her severest critics, despite their polarized evaluation, seem to agree that the nature of her art is enigmatic and often defies definition. In fact, Marvin Magalaner chooses the phrase "The Enigma of Katherine Mansfield" as the headline for the first chapter of his critical book *The Fiction of Katherine Mansfield*. Clare Hanson, echoing Magalaner, describes Mansfield's works as "allusive and elusive" ("Introduction" 9). Yet neither of them has ventured to interpret the constant use of fantasy as a part of this elusive style, much less, of her fictional technique.

Herbert Gold is one of the early critics who endeavor to define fantasy in terms of its nature and function as related to the art of short story. Fantasy, according to him, is "part of all the dreaming about alternatives which makes men human" (450). "Writers," he further argues, "have nevertheless been willing to employ their magic powers [of fantasy] as filters for faiths, concepts of law, visions of society" (451). He believes that fantasies, when successfully employed in a work of art, "seem more authentic and less unreal than the frights of everyday life," just as "stories" are "truer and more philosophical" than "history" (451–52). Nadine Gordimer holds a slightly different view. "Fantasy," she maintains, "is no more than a shift in angle" and "a wider lens on ultimate reality" (459–60). She further illustrates her point through an interesting metaphor:

> Fantasy is something that changes, merges, emerges, disappears as a pattern does viewed through the bottom of a glass. It is true for the moment when one looks down through the glass; but the same vision does not transform everything one sees, consistently throughout one's whole consciousness. (460)

Kathryn Hume in *Fantasy and Mimesis* opposes the arbitrary division between literature of mimesis and that of fantasy, for, she argues, all literature is the mixture of two impulses. One of them is mimesis—"the desire to imitate, to describe events, people, situations, and objects with such verisimilitude that others can share your experience." The other is fantasy—"the desire to change givens and alter reality— out of boredom, play, vision, longing for something lacking …" (20). Her definition is, therefore, more inclusive: "**Fantasy is any departure from consensus reality**, an impulse native to literature and manifested in innumerable variations, from monster to metaphor" (21).

However far apart their definitions may be, all of them agree that fantasy is an expression of discontent with both reality and the conventional approach to reality; it is a relatively new and freer means of probing the ultimate truth of life. Mansfield must have intuitively understood this while making the following comment, quoting Hegel:

> Why must thinking and existing be ever on two different planes? Why will the attempt of Hegel to transform subjective processes into objective world-processes not work out? "It is the special art and object of thinking to attain existence by quite other methods than that of existence itself." That is to say, reality cannot become the ideal, the dream; and it is not the business of the artist to grind an axe, to try to impose his vision of life upon the existing world. Art is not an attempt of the artist to reconcile existence with his vision; it is an attempt to create his own world in this world. (*Journal* 273)

This might serve, with a little adaptation, as Mansfield's modest artistic manifesto which juxtaposes the vision and the existence as two different perspectives of the same reality. To approach this reality by way of fantasy also implies a relative freedom of movement beyond the confines of existence. More specific to her art of story writing, the world of vision, or rather, of fantasy, is often dressed in the form of day-dreaming and role-playing, both of which are associated with the impulse to escape what is generally recognized as "reality."

For Mansfield, fantasy distinguishes itself not only as a unifying feature of her fiction, but also as a facet of her philosophical posture. To study it within the framework of her stories is a means to grasp the principle governing her art as well as her view on humanity. Yet unfortunately, this subject has not received its due attention over the long decades since her death. A number of her critics have been busy digging out the biographical information and interpreting her works in connection with the known events of her life. An equal number of books have been published in the area of comparative study, mainly examining the influence of Chekhov and the French symbolists on her art. There have been a few books which seek to isolate certain special qualities of her writing, occasionally touching upon the use of fantasy. Andrew Gurr's *Writers in Exile*, for instance, traces some aspects of Mansfield's experiences which contribute to the day-dreaming and role-playing quality of her characters. But it is essentially a study of the effect of exile on writers in general. Kate Fullbrook's *Katherine Mansfield* explores the fragmented self and **doppelganger** theme, which is a component of Mansfield's fantasy world. Her focus, nevertheless, is on the identification of Mansfield's feminist grounding with her constant attempt to transcend the boundaries of gender.

Of the limited number of studies which do set fantasy as their major critical concern, Cherry Hankin's "Fantasy and the Sense of an Ending in the Work of Katherine Mansfield" and *Katherine Mansfield and Her Confessional Stories* are the most extensive in scope. The latter, in particular, is a relatively systematic examination of the whole body of Mansfield's writing, tracing its development in light of her own emotional experiences. In this psycho-biographical study, Hankin draws and analyzes the parallel of Mansfield's emotional life and the development of fantasy, with a special emphasis on the method with which she "used her own dreams and disappointments as the raw material of fiction," and "employed all the resources of art to disguise, distance and shape her themes" (*Confessional Stories X*).

In this paper, I intend to draw on Hankin, to a certain extent, especially in relating the use of fantasy to the thematic pattern in her stories. Yet my scope is extended to the treatment of fantasy as a fictional technique by which Mansfield distinguishes herself as a great writer who succeeds "in assisting the English short story to a state of adult emancipation" (Bates 124). The function of fantasy is analyzed in connection with characterization. As Mansfield simultaneously believes in and doubts the possibility of a unified self, her characters are torn between their habitual indulgence in role-playing and a desire to distinguish and realize the true "self" from many "false" selves. The portrayal of their manifold experiences offers the reader multiple perspectives to probe their psychological depths. The use of fantasy, therefore, serves to achieve a psychological complexity.

This paper also discusses fantasy in relation to the imagery pattern and symbols. Mansfield has repeatedly renounced the analytical method in favor of a revelation through suggestive gestures in creative writing. Her world of fantasy is composed of a series of images rich in associative meanings. While her early works mainly center on a "dream figure," in later stories, her focal point shifts to the natural world for figurative expression. By presenting such images and symbols in the realm of fantasy, Mansfield unfolds a universally controversial aspect of life: an unquenchable desire for true love and artistic perfection mingled with a despair over the unattainability of them.

The three basic functions of fantasy as defined by Hume, i.e. additive, subtractive and contrastive, are all evident in Mansfield's fiction. This paper therefore also intends to explore their influence on her narrative structure. These three functions of fantasy serve to reinforce the progression of plot and heighten the effect of the thematic conflict by revealing, in different ways, the discrepancy and the resultant clash between fantasy and reality. The climactic clash usually ushers in the implied resolution to the conflict, as the character, in a sudden epiphanic moment, recognizes dream's inadequacy in altering reality, and, therefore, gains a new perception of life.

The recurrence of fantasy in Mansfield's stories is not incidental. The astonishing wealth of biographical information unearthed since her premature death has revealed several salient aspects of her life that can explain her indulgence in dreams, and the rest of this introductory chapter considers some of these.

Born in 1888 in Wellington, New Zealand, Katherine Mansfield, originally named Kathleen Beauchamp, has a childhood with a material abundance and a relative emotional aridity. She feels less loved than her siblings because she comes to the world at a time when the whole family is expecting a boy and heir. A precocious and sensitive child, she grows up with a feeling of oppression and threat of male dominance, first from the presence of her strong-willed father, and later also from the existence of Leslie, her only brother who has natural claim to every attention of the family. Having nobody to converse with except her grandmother, she becomes a "moody and resentful" girl with "a penetrating gaze" (Alpers 13). A lonely sufferer, little Kass, as Mansfield is called when young, seeks solace in her own kingdom of fantasy.

Later, Mansfield is able to re-create the affectionate family love denied her in her childhood in some of the tender parental figures, especially in her juvenilia. In "His Ideal," the earliest extant piece of writing according to Hankin (*Confessional Stories* 8), the central character is a delicate, elusive figure of a surrogate mother. She reveals herself to the young hero only in his illness, and her presence is unmistakably associated with the idea of purity:

> She was tall, and wore a long white robe, that shimmered like the moonbeams. Her white throat was bare.... She leant over him with a face full of tenderness and pity. And he, not knowing, ah! the poor little child, not knowing, stretched out his arms for her to take him up, and soothe him, and hold him to her breast. (Hankin *Confessional Stories* 8)

Yet this half-fairy woman refuses to step out of the realm of fantasy—she vanishes, leaving the "very very tired" child pining after her. When eventually she answers his call and returns, he, now an old man, feels "all his sorrows, his tears, and his bitterness fade away into the past" (9). Relaxing in her tender arms, he begins to realize that her name is Death.

"My Potplant," a piece composed a year later in 1904, repeats the pattern of an encounter with a magically attractive yet elusive mother figure, this time a woodswoman. But here, the heroine has abandoned the desire to fulfill her fantasy, acknowledging its unattainability. She decides, as the story concludes, that she "must step in the ranks and fight with the rest of the world" (Hankin *Confessional Stories* 14).

This childhood fantasy Mansfield occasionally carries over to some of her more mature works. The poor governess' adventure in Munich in "The Little Governess," for example, can obviously be attributed to her fantasized vision of a fellow traveler she meets on the train. The imaginative dear grandfather eventually turns out to be a disguised sexual predator, and the governess' dream of genuine parental affection is ruthlessly shattered.

Mansfield's habit of seeking alternatives in a dream world does not vanish with her childhood. In fact, her youthful and brief adult experiences continuously expand her capacity to fantasize. The recurrence of fantasy in her later works is largely a result of many antithetical forces operating in the course of her life, the first of which is her longing for an artistic freedom and the attendant fear of exile. Andrew Gurr, analyzing the state of writers in exile, makes the following comment:

> The exiled artist is like the rag which is tied in the middle of the rope used in a tug of war. He marks the still point between two straining forces. From one direction he is pulled by the sense of his own individuality which helped to make him an artist… From the other direction comes the tug of the unknown, the blank fear of the exile who has lost that sense of identity which comes from the feeling of belonging in a

community. By reacting against this community the artist knows his individuality. By exiling himself he loses it. If the two pulls are equal the rope under the rag will quiver but get nowhere. The artist likewise will strain in one direction, towards the realization of his individual vision, but find it impossible to move to it because of the counter-pull towards the communal identity which has shaped that individuality and without which he has no identity, or therefore individuality, of any kind. (33)

This is exactly the situation in which Katherine Mansfield is placed during her brief career as a creative writer.

At the time of her birth, New Zealand as a separate British colony is hardly fifty years old, and most of its residents still regard Britain as their "home." As the dominant social force is the mercantile class to which the Beauchamps belong, bourgeois values are the norms used to judge one's social success. Mansfield matures as an artist much earlier than as a woman, a situation uncongenial to the pace of Wellington's social development—a rapid material progress accompanied by a relatively slow cultural advancement. When in late 1906 she is urged home after a three-year education in Queen's College, London, she feels the banal Wellington provincial life a complete nightmare. She has a haunting fear that her young artistic talent will be smothered in a land which does not inspire nor encourage the Muses. A journal entry dated October 21, 1907 is very indicative of her mood:

> Here in my room, I feel as though I was in London. In London! To write the word makes me feel that I could burst into tears. Isn't it terrible to love anything so much? I don't care at all for men, but **London**—it is life I am longing to consort with my superiors. What is it with me? Am I absolutely nobody, but merely inordinately vain? I do not know.... but I am most fearfully unhappy. That is all. I am so unhappy that I wish I was dead—yet I should be mad to die when I have not yet lived **at all**. (21)

This is a feeble yet angry voice crying out for artistic freedom, a voice afraid of being swallowed in an immense sea of bourgeois conventionality. Later in the same entry, Mansfield starts to fantasize life in a culturally superior society:

> I like to appear… entirely at my ease, conscious of my importance, which in my estimation is unlimited, affable and very receptive. I like to appear slightly condescending, very much **du grand monde**, and to be the center of interest. (22)

Her youthful fantasy, however, does not come true, for London is slow in appreciating her value. Her first collection of stories *In a German Pension* (1911), the result of a series of emotional whirlwinds, is lukewarmly received, attracting comments about her as being "cleverly observant" (Alpers 129). The very next year brings about a little turning in her career when she starts to live with John Middleton Murry, a fledging critic and editor, between whose little magazine *Rhythm* and A. P. Orage's *New Age*, Mansfield finds a space to display her artistic talent.

However, the Murrys are just wandering on the fringe of the London literary elite. It is evident, by the following two facts, that they do not belong to the mainstream of the Bohemian coterie. First, most of their close friends, as Gurr points out, are themselves exiles (39). Beatrice Hasting, once Mansfield's mentor, is originally from South Africa; Beatrice Campbell, her confidante, is from Ireland; Koteliansky, a Russian; and Frieda Lawrence, with whom they are once intimate, is banished from her German home. Secondly, the Bloomsburies never consider them their social equals. Virginia Woolf, for example, records slightingly in her diary dated October 11, 1917, of her first meeting with Mansfield. She describes Mansfield as "common," "cheap," stinking like a "civet cat that had taken to street walking" (*Diary* Vol. I 58). This acid sharpness is later softened when the Woolfs discover the shining intellect hidden beneath the surface. The class barrier between them, nevertheless, is still there. The Murrys continue to be categorized into the literary underworld in the Woolfs' estimation. This sense of repulsion is probably mutual, for according to Murry in his autobiography *Between Two Worlds*, Mansfield also feels uneasy in the fashionable London literary salons:

> A silly, unreal evening. Pretty rooms and pretty people, pretty coffee, and cigarettes
> out of a silver tankard. A sort of sham Meredith atmosphere lurking… I was wretched.
> I have nothing to say to "charming" women. I feel like a cat among tigers. (290)

These impressions Mansfield is to translate successfully into some of her stories. The pretentious and shallow Norman Knights in "Bliss" and Isabel's boisterous artist friends in "Marriage A La Mode" evidently reflect the lifestyle of the London Bohemians whom she has come to know. Behind this crusty mask of dignity, it is not hard to detect the trace of inferiority complex deep-rooted in this "little Colonial walking in the London garden patch," who is "allowed to look, perhaps, but not to linger" (*Journal* 157). Her voice sounds terribly alone and uncertain, and her financial strain further prevents her from "mixing with the frivolous, carefree elements of the society" (Hormasji 48).

This is Mansfield's position during 1908–1923. She has bid farewell to Wellington because of its uncongeniality to her temperament. Yet her fourteen years of willing exile in Europe, especially in Britain, does not erase her feeling as an outsider. "She had wrenched herself free from her native country," as Sylvia Berkman suggests in her illuminating critical biography of Mansfield, "to find the country of her hope and faith crumble. She could not return; she had passed beyond the point of return. She must seek or make a world now within herself" (146).

This "world within herself" Mansfield is soon to create. The New Zealand stories, generally acclaimed her best, are the fruits borne out of her solitude in and disillusionment with the actual world. Many critics have over-stressed the function of her brother's death in her decision to write about their common home country. By no means is her desire to "lift that mist from my people and let them be seen" (*Letters* 75) a willful impulse. The land she so beautifully and romantically depicts is not the New Zealand which she quits in 1908. It is, instead, her extended childhood fantasy which has now risen beyond any destructive power of the real world, with its ugly spots blurred away from a safe distance, both in time and in space.

The second antithetical force which contributes to the recurrence of fantasy stems from Mansfield's split emotional life, which, like a pendulum, constantly swings between a dream of a harmonious married life and an attachment to a lesbian sisterhood. Mansfield's attitude towards men has been ambivalent from the beginning, and her disapproval of them finds its best expression in the themes of excessive male sexual desires and the attendant childbirth trauma experienced by their female partners. As early as 1907 she has started to demonstrate clear lesbian tendencies by being involved in some passionate affairs with two Wellington girls. These adolescent anecdotes are only a prelude to her delicate triangular relationships with John Middleton Murry and Ida Constance Baker, which are to last for eleven years of her adult life. Mansfield's marriage is by no means a peaceful one, and her habitual self-dramatization has made every hour of her emotional life a moment of crisis. When separation from Murry is necessitated, first by different working habits and mutual feelings of depression, and later by her illness, Mansfield's moods alternate between a passionate love and an equally passionate hate. She ascribes their emotional clashes to their reversal of roles in life:

> We had been **children** to each other, openly confessed children, telling each other everything, and each depending equally upon the other. Before that, I had been the man and he had been the woman, and he had been called upon to make no real efforts. He had never really "supported" me…. Then this illness, getting worse and worse, and turning me into a woman…. He stood it marvelously. (*Scrapbook* 147–48)

It is evident now that the tragic element in the Mansfield-Murry relationship is but a result of the conflict between Mansfield's intellectual self and the physical self. While her intellectual self remains vigorous and masculine, her illness has reduced her physical self into a fragile and dependent woman. The situation is further aggravated when Murry fails to work out a corresponding change.

During Mansfield's fits of emotional depression with Murry, Ida Constance Baker, alias Leslie Moore, is conveniently called upon to "play off one against the other" (Hankin *Confessional Stories* 166). Mansfield's need for L. M., however, is only periodic and her journals and letters are dotted with spiteful comments, describing their relationship as "the bitterest enemies imaginable" (*Journal* 153). Her complaints about L. M. cannot be easily explained away as merely a sign of self-dramatization or a gesture to assure Murry of his primary importance, as L. M. believes in her *Memories* (234, 236). L. M.'s intellectual inadequacy has doomed her an unsuitable companion for Mansfield in literary intercourse, and more crucial is her unquestioning loyalty which irritates Mansfield, because it reminds her of Murry's weakness.

Having experienced love with both sexes and finding it unsatisfactory, Mansfield again has to turn within herself and construct the kingdom of ideal love in the realm of fantasy. "Something Childish But Very Natural," a story written in 1913 when she is still happy with Murry, reflects some of her early ideas of love. It is a tale about two adolescent lovers, Henry and Edna, who meet in a commuting train and fall passionately in love. Yet Edna refrains from any physical contacts with Henry for fear that their relationship "would be all changed" and they "wouldn't be children any more" (*Something Childish and Other Stories* 145). The heroine, or rather Mansfield herself, believes that love can be eternal as long as the innocence is intact. In this story, Mansfield has already hinted at the destructive effect of the daily intimacy, for, at the end of the story, Edna fails to show up at the little house they plan to share.

In Mansfield's later stories, when she matures both as a woman and as an artist, this pattern of ideal childlike innocent love gradually disappears and some of her characters involved in emotional crises start to seek solace in a different form of fantasy. They aspire for a marriage grounded fundamentally in mutual understanding and sentiments, like Linda Burnell in "Prelude." They desire, though to no avail, to share genuine feelings with their own sex; and sometimes, like Bertha Young in "Bliss," they shift their sexual roles under different circumstances. They no longer cling to dreams as the substitute for reality. This relative independence allows them a certain degree of freedom to move between the worlds of subjective vision and objective reality.

In addition to these two-way pulls accompanying Mansfield's entire life, World War I is also largely responsible for the tendency to "turn within" in her works. During the initial stage of the War, the Murrys are still roaming, undisturbed, in their self-contained world of letters, with a naive belief that "the War...was not **for** anything—anything of importance" (Murry *Between the Two Worlds* 299). Mansfield is soon shocked into awareness of the War's personal impact on her, first by her three-week detention in Paris because of the bombardment, which drastically worsens her lung condition; secondly, by the death of her only brother Leslie and many of Murry's friends who never return from the battlefields. The Murrys, no longer able to feign an indifference, begin to question the meaning of the War. Mansfield, in fact, cannot help feeling outraged at Virginia Woolf's cold omission of War in her writing (*Letters to Murry* 381).

With the War raging on, the established body of truth collapses before them with nothing to fill the void; the old value system is blown asunder and the new one yet to come. If the fear of exile and the emotional crises cast doubtful shadows on Mansfield's faith in humanity, the War has crumbled her view of the universe, leaving her probing her own way in darkness. The result of this decay of uniform belief is as Berkman indicates:

> The seeking mind was driven in upon itself, to construct among the fragments its own vision. We have thus the flowering of individual expression, shaped by individual temperament out of individual experience, to be tested as true or false by individual temperament and experience. (150)

If there is still truth to be sought, it has to be approached from a new perspective now. This new perspective to truth, expressed in individual vision and voice, consequently assumes the form of fantasy in Mansfield's world of fiction.

CHAPTER II

FANTASY AND CHARACTERIZATION

In *Fantasy and Mimesis*, Kathryn Hume divides fantasy into three major categories according to the different ways it relates to plot and characterization. The first, according to her, is "action-oriented fantasy" where "the departure from reality generates action." The second is "character-based fantasy," which often assumes the form of stories told by "non-human narrators." The third, "idea-fantasy," revolves around a central fantastic idea which may affect, if not generate, the action of the characters (159–62). A careful reading of Katherine Mansfield's works shows that her use of fantasy, especially as a device to aid characterization, sometimes eludes Hume's classification. In most of her stories, the setting is strictly mimetic, and her characters are obviously not fairy figures despite their dreamy existence. The realm of dream is seldom, if ever, extended to that of action. This virtually precludes any kinship to Hume's first two categories. It is true that most of her protagonists do indulge in fantastic ideas, but fantasy does not necessarily change their course of life or drastically affect their relationships with other people. The character-portrayal depends, therefore, not upon their action but upon their mind process.

Mansfield resorts to two basic inter-related forms of fantasy for characterization—role-playing and day-dreaming, both of which adhere to her concept of "self." In a feministic study of Mansfield, Kate Fullbrook has noticed the alternative doubt and faith in her attitude towards a unified self. Mansfield's journal has also reiterated the "deep but resisted desire to believe in a continuous self that holds the possibility of release from roles, masks and fragmentation into a moment of pure being" (Fullbrook 19). In an entry dated late April 1920, Mansfield playfully raises the question of the nature of self:

True to oneself! What self? Which of my many—well really, that's what it looks
like coming to—hundreds of selves? For what with complexes and repressions and
reactions and vibrations and reflections, there are moments when I feel I am nothing
but the small clerk of some hotel without a proprietor, who has all his work cut out to
enter the names and hand the keys to the willful guests. (205)

While recognizing the existence of multi-selves in the human psyche, Mansfield
does not fall into utter despair in her quest for a consistent and unified self. To this
quest she attributes "the rage for confession" in literature:

… there are signs that we are intent as never before on trying to puzzle out, to live by,
our own particular self. Der Mensch muss frei sein – free, disentangled, single. Is it
not possible that… our persistent yet mysterious belief in a self which is continuous
and permanent…., untouched by all we acquire and all we shed, pushes a green spear
through the dead leaves and through the mould, thrusts a scaled bud through years of
darkness until, one day, the light discovers it and shakes the flower free and—we are
alive—we are flowering for our moment upon the earth? This is the moment which,
after all, we live for… (*Journal* 205)

This flowering moment of self-discovery, phrased as "epiphany" and "moment of
being" by later writers such as James Joyce and Virginia Woolf, is infinitesimal
and evanescent according to Mansfield, whereas the state of confusion in face
of a fragmented self is universal and lingering. Identity becomes a relative and
vulnerable term when self is "multiple, shifting, non-consecutive" and "without
essence" (Fullbrook 17). As each of the multiple selves is elusive and fleeting,
a relatively concrete and consistent image should be constructed, artificially, to
assume one's social function as well as to protect one from utter fragmentation.
Very early on in her career as a writer, Mansfield has become aware of the necessity
for a public self, "a mask" in her vocabulary, which, she repeatedly warns Murry,
cannot be lowered even when alone (*Letters to Murry* 94).

This concept of self explains both the genesis of many of her characters indulging in role-playing and her method of characterization through a revelation of role clashes. It will be an over-simplification to apply labels such as "true" and "false" to our evaluation of these split selves as they appear in her fantasy scenes. Each of them, equally representative of and true to the character, reflects an aspect, however insignificant, of the individual and contributes to the totality of his being.

Unlike Thomas Hardy's Jude and Eustacia, Mansfield's heroes and heroines do not often feel the **acute** pain of dislocation in their social environment, nor do they wrestle with their souls in quest of religious or moral truth, like Dinah Morris in George Eliot's *Adam Bede*. Their fundamental unhappiness or disappointment frequently originates from their awareness of the conflicts between their multitude of selves, or of the discrepancies between their intuitive nature and the expected social functions. The battle is fought, therefore, not against a malicious God or a vile society but against the enemy of self; not in the vast world of natural phenomena but within the narrow confines of the human psyche; not through a series of external physical actions but through a gradual revelation of individual consciousness. As Mansfield's literary endeavors evidently concentrate on the explorations of the mind process, plot is deemed an inadequate means for character portrayal. The traditional way of characterization through exposure of external crisis has to be replaced by a new method.

This new method Mansfield is soon to discover. She introduces into most of her stories the technique of fantasy, a means not only of probing her characters' psychological depths by revealing their internal crisis in the form of day-dreaming, but also of exploring their different perspectives of life through the various roles they assume. The epiphany, or the moment of insight, in their quest for a "fundamental" self, is a moment of crystallization and sublimity. But it is also a moment of terror and "collapse," because to be able to decipher the myth of "self" is to lose faith in it, as Elaine Showalter asserts in *Literature of Their Own* (247). These flashes of insight or moments of revelation, with their paradoxical implications, consequently become focal points in Mansfield's characterization.

A great number of Mansfield's protagonists are self-indulgent role-players. They love to conjure up their dream worlds, each inhabited by an assumed personality, where they can evade the unpleasantness of reality and metaphorically fulfill their secret aspirations. To this large group belongs the sentimental heroine in "The Little Governess, " a story tinged with the author's "bitter mood of humiliation and self-condemnation" after a short-lived romance with Francis Carco (Hankin *Confessional Stories* 97–98).

"The Little Governess," on a first reading, is a story focusing on the worn-out theme of innocence abroad, and its heroine just another of Mansfield's pathetic characters who "cannot distinguish between truth and wishfulfilment" (Hankin 98). A second reading, however, reveals a deeper truth than meets the eye. Through the portrayal of the different roles that the governess plays and their ultimate clash, Mansfield creates a subtle and complex character whose apparent innocence is partly a gesture of evading adult responsibilities and partly a disguised desire for masculine love and protection. The first symptom of this role-playing syndrome is her constant shrinking into the cocoon of a prolonged childhood, a state Nariman Hormasji describes as "adult infantilism" occasionally "bordering on neurosis" (89).

She starts to betray her greedy dependency in the meeting at the Governess Bureau, a pretextual episode in which she absorbs the information offered by the lady in charge with a childish, unquestioning attitude. When the long journey to Germany unfolds, she conveniently slips into the role of a child who craves for a parental love and care:

> It had been nice in the Ladies' Cabin. The stewardess was so kind and changed her money for her and tucked up her feet. She lay on one of the hard pink-sprigged couches and watched the other passengers, friendly and natural, pinning their hats to the bolsters, taking off their boots and skirts, opening dress-cases and arranging mysterious rustling little packages, tying their heads up in veils before lying down. Thud, thud, thud, went the steady screw of the steamer. The stewardess pulled a green shade over the light and sat down by the stove, her skirt turned back over her knees,

a long piece of knitting on her lap... "I like travelling very much," thought the little governess. She smiled and yielded to the warm rocking. (*Bliss and Other Stories* 240)

Here the nameless governess evades the seriousness of her first journey into adulthood by simulating that she is travelling under parental protection. In her fantasy, she evidently interprets the routine service of the stewardess as a sign of motherly care. The cabin, with its coziness, is associated with a cradle, and even the couch where she chooses to rest is pink-colored, suggestive of the setting of a dream world. Her attention to the trivials around her also indicates a sense, albeit feigned, of curiosity typically seen in a child who tends to observe the world uncritically.

The governess still clings to her infantilism, after the ship lands, by literally acting upon the advice given by the lady at the Bureau—"it's better to mistrust people at first rather than trust them" (239). She becomes excessively wary as she steps out of the cabin. When a porter approaches her and grabs her luggage, she hastily concludes that he is "a robber" (241). Then later, she again plays the role of a little girl ignoring the rules of the adult world by willfully refusing to pay due tips to both the railway porter and the hotel waiter. But by feigning to be a child she is not to be exempt from the penalty—she is punished in both cases, like many erring Victorian heroines, for her transgression of the adult law.

The shift of the governess' role, in the middle of the narrative, from an uncritical child to a self-conscious young woman, indicates Mansfield's attempt to add complexity to her characterization. The transitional moment is also a moment of role clash, through which the author catches and subsequently conveys to the reader the "fundamental" character of the governess as far more subtle than just an "innocent abroad." Her first glance at her travelling companion—her fantasized grandfather, for example, immediately reveals that her interest in him is not completely asexual:

How spick and span he looked for an old man. He wore a pearl pin stuck in his black tie and a ring with a dark red stone on his little finger; the tip of a white silk handkerchief showed in the pocket of his double-breasted jacket. Somehow, altogether, he was really nice to look at. (246)

It is not until she discovers his physical attraction that she starts to adjust her attitude—her role as a child begins to concede to that of a young woman. Aware of the old man's attention, she "peeps at him through her long lashes" (246), and "dimples at him" (252), "blushing a deep pink colour that spreads slowly over her cheeks and makes her blue eyes look almost black" (246). Her self-dramatization of her youth and charm sounds altogether sentimental:

Alas! How tragic for a little governess to possess hair that made one think of tangerines and marigolds, of apricots and tortoiseshell cats and champagne! Not even the dark ugly clothes could disguise her soft beauty. (247)

She further excites his interest by continuously responding to his attention. She soon makes him her confidant and pours out her life story flirtatiously. When he hesitantly suggests the possibility of "taking a little holiday," she responds, again flirtatiously, that she cannot oblige him because she is "alone" (249). During their tour of Munich, she allows him to take her arm, walk closely by her side, and share one umbrella. Her speech and manner are unmistakably associated with that of a woman intoxicated by the dream of love. As if afraid of her first emotional experience, the governess persistently calls upon her role of an innocent "child" to justify her behavior as a coquettish young woman. Just as she has expressed her awakened sexual longing in a disguise of a need for parental protection, so she fantasizes his amorous attention as a form of grandfatherly love. The following monologue betrays one of her attempts at self-justification:

Perhaps [emphasis mine] the flush that licked his cheeks and lips was a flush of rage that anyone so young and tender should have to travel alone and unprotected through the night. Who knows he was not murmuring in his sentimental German fashion: "**Ja, es ist eine Tragoedie!** Would to God I were the child's grandpapa!" (247)

She likewise dismisses her own coquetry as signs of gratitude for the strawberries, ice creams, and the tour around Munich. The terms "grandpapa" and "fairy grandfather" appear with a greater frequency as the governess' attachment to the old man grows. But her "grandfather," unfortunately, proves to be merely a creation of her fantasy. When in his ugly apartment he "presses against her his hard old body" (259) and forces a kiss on her virginal lips, the world of fantasy dissolves before her, and the only response she is capable of uttering is: "It was a dream! It wasn't true" (259)! Hankin has pointed out the irony which overlays the narrative—"one with so much to learn as the little governess has no business to be starting out as a teacher" (*Confessional Stories* 99). The irony of the story contains yet another fold: while deceptive veils are established as the face of reality, the bare truth is presented in a dream-like uncertainty.

The moment of crisis for the governess is the one in which her two split selves ultimately confront each other. Her assumed role of a child lulls her to a state of dependency where she can demand attention and service without incurring the attendant responsibilities. Yet the other self, the role of a young maturing woman, forces her to face the consequences of her own emotional adventures. As each of the two roles represents a facet of the little governess as a complex character, their very irreconcilability adds to her psychological depth.

F. M. Perry, one of Mansfield's contemporary critics, comments in *The Art of Story-writing* that Mansfield's most successful literary projects are those in which the characters are "put into reciprocal relation" (213). Twenty-five years later, Sylvia Berkman also assesses favorably Mansfield's technique of providing her characters with "a space… to grow," for they can be better portrayed through the way they respond to their social environment (200). In this sense, the characterization in "The Little Governess" is incomplete, for its heroine is allowed only a limited degree of freedom of movement. In addition, by making hers the only interpreting consciousness, the world of fantasy sometimes loses touch with that of reality because of the lack of reciprocal responses.

"The Little Governess" is, nevertheless, only one of Mansfield's early experiments in characterization, for stories preceding it, including those collected in *In a German Pension*, are, at their best, character sketches. In the earlier pieces, the protagonists are generally connected to each other and to their entire social environment only through the immediate event which constitutes the skinny plot, and sometimes they simply dwell in complete isolation, like the dreamy heroine in "Something Childish but Very Natural."

In her later stories, Mansfield is able to explore the "inner man" through a fuller revelation of the interaction between fantasy and reality in a more complex web of human relationships. In "Bliss," for example, although Bertha's consciousness still dominates the narrative voice, the characterization relies heavily upon her fantasized vision of, and response to, a complex group of people, including her husband Harry, a mystic and elusive woman Pearl, and their eccentric Bohemian friends. In "Je Ne Parle Pas Français," the characterization of Mouse is basically achieved through two men's individual reaction to her. The reader's judgment of the character and situation is continuously adjusted and manipulated as the two versions of Mouse keep on correcting each other and the two heroes, Dick and "I", move in and out of the fantasy world. "The Man Without a Temperament," on the other hand, witnesses a new technique in characterization. The choice of a hotel as the setting of the narrative not only establishes a wider social horizon but also allows the hero, a man caught in the miserable dilemma of life, to be observed and portrayed from multiple points of view. Yet none of them exceeds, either in complexity of human relationships or in depth of characterization, Mansfield's semi-autobiographical work "Prelude," the longest and one of the most discussed stories in her canon.

In "Prelude," Mansfield weaves her fabric of truth out of her familiar theme— theme of "one character's private or ideal vision of self" clashing with "his or her perception of the physical world" or "a private vision... threatened by the conventional duties demanded by a family role" (Peterson 387). In this story, the author's predominant technique of characterization is again through a revelation of split identities and the attendant phenomenon of day-dreaming, but this time against a more extensive social canvas. Unlike the heroine in "The Little Governess" whose crisis is explored through a dramatic event—a journey to Germany and an encounter with a stranger—the characters in "Prelude" obtain their insights into self through their involvement in and reaction to ordinary family life. Each of the roles they assume, both in fantasy and in reality, not only contributes to their view of life as individual beings, but also exposes their attitudes towards each other as social beings. What has held them from utter fragmentation is their capability to dream about alternatives and to accept life as it is simultaneously.

The story has Linda Burnell as its central character, around whom the family web is woven. She is a wife, a mother, a daughter and a sister all at the same time, yet she finds it hard to harmonize these roles because of their contradictory functions. Her dependency upon her mother Mrs. Fairfield for both physical assistance and mental sustenance renders her an incompetent mother, and her repulsion for child-bearing threatens to jeopardize her marriage to Stanley. Her role as a wife, on the other hand, makes her relationship with her pretty and unmarried sister Beryl a subtle one. What has engaged Mansfield's major attention in the story, nevertheless, is not the clashes between these public functions, but the discrepancies between these roles and Linda's private ideal of self. The seeking of this ideal self, that is, her soul's travail, also constitutes the process of her characterization.

Linda's split selves find their first expression in her divided roles as mother public and mother private. As mother public, she provides, although with little genuine affection, her three daughters with a relatively affluent and comfortable life. As mother private, she sees her children as irrelevant events forced upon her from without and accidental trophies of a shameful "sexual guerrilla war" (Fullbrook 85). Ironically, the mother public, who mainly dwells in reality, is remote, vague and elusive, whereas the mother private, who largely roams in the realm of fantasy, is tangible and concrete. While the former labors to sustain the weight of a mask, the latter longs to shake free from it.

Linda's indifference to the children is made evident at the very beginning of the story when the Burnell household is planning for a move. The metaphorical significance of opening a story with a house-moving scene is addressed with great insight in Fullbrook's critical book:

> Moving house is itself used as a metaphor for the possibility of change as the characters are temporarily dislodged from their habits and set roles…. It most certainly suggests—an occasion of defamiliarisation and estrangement from previous selves and circumstances that prompts a series of movements of self-awareness for the characters. (67–68)

It is with an eager anticipation for a new mood under altered circumstances that Linda gets herself involved in this hectic domestic maneuver. One of her gestures of farewell to the old identities is her decision to leave behind with the Samuel Josephs her two daughters, Kezia and Lottie, whom she declares as not included in her "absolute necessities" (*Bliss and Other Stories* 1).

When the girls eventually arrive at their new home after an exhausting night journey, Linda does not "even open her eyes to see" (12). Yet her attempt to bid farewell to the past only results in the return of all the old "headaches." The very first night she spends in her new house she dreams a strange dream. She is walking with her father through a paddock when they discover a bird, "a tiny ball of fluff" at her feet. The bird, to her gentle stroke, begins to swell and finally grows into "a baby with a big naked head and a gaping bird-mouth, opening and shutting." She wakes with terror only to find Stanley "standing by the windows ratting the Venetian blind up" (20). The dream reflects her waking fear—while she can accept baby as an idea as long as it is kept at a distance like the tiny fluffy bird, the concrete presence of a growing child who threatens her freedom is to her a complete nightmare. Her dream version of life, where she shrinks at the sight of a swelling baby, corresponds to her real-life experience in which the two rival mother roles clash.

Linda's ambivalent feelings towards motherhood is reflected in her attitude especially towards Kezia, the most thoughtful and sensitive of the three girls. A very revealing episode is her accidental meeting with Kezia in the garden, the only real contact between the mother and daughter. When Kezia raises the question regarding the aloe tree, Linda is caught before she has time to put on the mask of indifference:

> "Mother, what is it?" asked Kezia.
>
> Linda looked up at the fat swelling plant with its cruel leaves and fleshy stem. High above them, as though becalmed in the air, and yet holding so fast to the earth it grew from, it might have had claws instead of roots. The curving leaves seemed to be hiding something; the blind stem cut into the air as if no wind could ever shake it.
>
> "That is an aloe, Kezia," said her mother.
>
> "Does it ever have any flowers?"
>
> "Yes, Kezia," and Linda smiled down at her, and half shut her eyes. "Once every hundred years." (34)

Here Linda can no longer evade Kezia's demand for interpretive guidance. While Linda's response is brief and languid, her meaningful smile supplies what is left unsaid—an admiration for the aloe as a symbol of feminine strength and defensive power mingled with a repulsion for its "swelling," a gesture of sexual aggression. More significant is Linda's mixed feelings for the tree's ability to blossom. Its rare yet noble moment of flowering reminds her simultaneously of the sublimity of human reproductive power and the child-birth trauma she has endured and will continue to endure in life. For the first time in the story, the two split mother roles find their unification in the contemplation of the aloe, and her realm of fantasy overlaps that of reality. The alienated mother and daughter, through their common interest in this strange plant, betray signs of willingness to share. Although too young to enter the complicated mood of her mother, Kezia must have intuitively understood this significant moment of real spiritual connection, as a child and as a female. By presenting the two sides of Linda which imply both feminine strength and feminine weakness, Mansfield creates a three-dimensional character who acts and reacts, not upon concepts, but from the dilemma of her complicated experience.

Linda's fragmented personality as a psychologically complex character is also explored through her love-hate relationship with Stanley. Constantly in conflict are her assigned role of a bourgeois wife and the private role of a woman. While the former is largely reflected in the existence of a husband, the latter reacts uneasily to her social mask. It is the private woman in Linda that Mansfield manages to bring into sharp focus. Outwardly, Linda participates in Stanley's middle-class complacency and accepts, though listlessly, his bourgeois value system, best described as a "Gatsby complex" for social success, to borrow one of Richard Peterson's apt phrases (389). But there is another self, a self distorted to the verge of extinction by pressures of a routinized life, yet still struggling to break loose from the confines of a conventional marriage. This is the Linda we find on the second morning after she settles in her new house. With the slam of the front door which signals Stanley's departure for work, Linda's role as a wife terminates for the time being and she immediately slips into her other self. Even before her sense of novelty wears off, she has already developed symptoms of repulsion for her new environment:

> All the furniture had found a place—all the paraphernalia—as she expressed it. Even the photographs were on the mantelpiece and the medicine bottles on the shelf above the washstand. Her clothes lay across a chair—her outdoor things, a purple cape and a round hat with a plume in it. Looking at them she wished that she was going away from the house, too. And she saw herself driving away from them all in a little buggy, driving away from everybody and not even waving. (20–21)

The very orderliness, fitting her mood only when she is assuming the personality of Stanley's wife, now annoys and suffocates her. When her public role dissolves with his departure, the private self becomes actively engaged in the dreaming about alternatives. If she "gave herself up and was quiet. ... silent, motionless," she fears, "THEY"—the mysterious sinister forces which haunt her, would gorge her up tracelessly (25).

This restless and dreamy Linda swiftly retreats into her mask when Stanley returns from work. She responds to his kiss with due warmth but soon diverts his attention to the children. She tolerates his animalistic appetite for food and avoids his further attempts at intimacy by simply walking away to watch the moon. Yet the moon, which, in her fantasy, with its remoteness and radiance, points to the potentiality of transcendence, if not escape, paradoxically makes her shiver in reality. Feeling chilled, she decides to "come away from the window and sit down upon the ottoman beside Stanley" (40), the man she partly desires and partly rejects. If the aloe scene has exhibited the only moment of an intuitive communication between Linda and Kezia, this climactic moon scene suggests the surrender of Linda's private self to the role of Stanley's wife, a defeat of fantasy by reality. Thus, as the two roles alternatively dominate Linda's mood, her life is divided between long hours of silence and some flashing moments of revolt.

This divisibility of life, made overt through fantasy scenes, offers us an opportunity to observe and judge the character of Linda both objectively, as she performs her role of wife, and subjectively, as we are ushered into her private thoughts. What has kept this divisibility under control is Linda's state of passive acceptance. While the expected pattern of conduct of a middle-class wife suppresses the constant surge of the hidden self, her ability to find relief and solace in dreams makes the reality less hard to endure. It is this divisibility, and therefore, the absurdity, of life that makes her "laugh silently" in her night vigil:

> "What am I guarding myself for so preciously? I shall go on having children and Stanley will go on making money and the children and the gardens will grow bigger and bigger, with whole fleets of aloes in them for me to choose from." (62–63)

The divisibility of life is also illustrated in the divisibility of the Burnell household. It is separated, by gender as well as by temperament, into two worlds which coexist and repel each other simultaneously. Stanley, the Burnell patriarch, is characterized with a complete reliance upon external values for interpretation of reality. To him there is no other truth than that which is contained in the material. The female world in "Prelude," on the contrary, rejects the orthodox male version of truth by redefining reality as something subjective and, therefore, possibly beyond the realm of matter.

Most of the Burnell women are bestowed with the ability of day-dreaming, a gift naturally affiliated with their habit of role-playing. As day-dreams function to filter the data of reality before it is absorbed into their consciousness, the selective process reveals, therefore, part of their personalities. Linda's vision of the aloe tree as "a ship" rowing "far away over the top of the garden trees" (60), for instance, suggests her rebellious nature as a woman despite the expected social roles. Alice's rehearsal of the "most marvelous retorts… for questions that she knew would never be put to her" (54), likewise, betrays a servile and vain personality. Her attempts to maintain integrity are executed through a discriminating attitude towards members of the Burnell household according to their different positions in the family.

Beryl Fairfield's dream is also indicative of her character. Her narcissistic moments of fantasy in mirror-gazing, for example, convey the surfaced fear of an ultimate falsity of existence. While the reflection in the looking glass seems to her less false but more elusive, the actual self which makes the mirror image is what she absolutely abhors:

> What had that creature in the glass to do with her, and why was she staring? She dropped down to one side of her bed and buried her face in her arms.
> "Oh," she cries, "I am so miserable—so frightfully miserable. I know that I'm silly and spiteful and vain; I'm always acting a part. I'm never my real self for a moment." (68)

The sense of falsity presents itself in the different roles Beryl assumes in the Burnell household. When with Stanley, she fantasizes a usurpation of Linda's part by being cleverly coquettish. To Kezia and Alice, she exercises her imaginative power of a mentor and matron to revenge her humiliation of being a dependent to her sister's family. To Linda, she is a sibling rival for the mother's affection.

These roles and the dreams attached to them combine to establish, from different perspectives, her ultimate personality as a restless and wayward woman whose unhappiness in life is largely the result of the failure of finding a "true" self.

Beryl's dream also reflects a fear that many of Mansfield's unmarried heroines share—the fear of a social denial because of their inability to acquire a husband. Like the fidgety Mouse in "Je Ne Parle Pas Français," and the neurotic music teacher in "The Singing Lesson," Beryl counts on marriage for assurance of personal salvation. Her choice of a young man as the center of her dream world to alleviate the anguish of rivaling selves establishes her as an antithesis to Linda. While Beryl's character is defined by direct expression of passion, Linda's world can only be accessed through intuitive understanding.

Hankin has drawn our attention to the different motives for day-dreaming as found in "Prelude:"

> Fantasizing or day-dreaming is common to Kezia, Linda, Beryl and Doady. All four youthful characters are sharply differentiated... For Kezia and Linda, fantasizing is an almost involuntary activity, one in which some external object or event causes repressed anxieties to rise to the surface of their minds. But for Beryl and Doady it is a conscious indulgence which allows them to escape from daily routine and gratify, at least in imagination, their unfulfilled wishes. (*Confessional Stories* 126)

Hankin's observation is precise but incomplete. To all of these characters, fantasy is not just an impulse to escape the monotony of daily routine, or to substitute it with an imaginative experience. It is also, because of its constant and habitual intrusion onto life, an inseparable part of their existence. The description of fantasy becomes, accordingly, a part of characterization. When dream enters reality, the characters' capacity to live is significantly expanded with this added dimension. As the demarcation between existence and imagination is made tenuous, their subjective world in turn grows more complex, and so does the characterization.

In *Aspects of the Novel*, E. M. Forster describes fictional characters either as "flat" or "round." "Flat characters," he argues, "are constructed around a single idea or quality;" whereas, round characters are marked with a readiness "for an extended life" (83). The Burnells are believable because they possess exactly this rich potentiality for an extended experience. In Kezia, for instance, the reader discovers indefinite possibilities for life. These possibilities are explored through a description of her fantasy world which links her with the divided adult world. Although the story is narrated from multiple points of view, many of the episodes are actually filtered through Kezia's consciousness. As the filtering process is both personal and selective, Kezia's choice of perspective reflects her potential character development. Saralyn Daly concludes convincingly, after a careful observation of her two days' behavior in "Prelude," that Kezia is affiliated to the grandmother, Mrs. Fairfield, through their common love for order (70–71).

Mrs. Fairfield is depicted as the one, next to Stanley, who is devoid of the ability to sentimentalize situations. The ideas which she cherishes are mostly associated with utilitarian values. While, for example, Linda is contemplating the aloe, ruminating over a possibility of freedom and chastity which the tree symbolizes, Mrs. Fairfield's thoughts run to the prospective of a good season for fruit jam. In some of the most telling episodes, Kezia exhibits certain traits which unmistakably remind us of Mrs. Fairfield. But ironically, Kezia's efforts to imitate grandmother's practicality are executed through the medium of fantasy. When left behind with the Samuel Josephs, she searches through the deserted old house for anything of value, as Mrs. Fairfield would normally do in similar situations. One of her findings is "a pill box black and shiny outside and red in, holding a blob of cotton wool" (6). But its use she can only associate with a fantastic idea of "keeping a bird's egg" (6). In the same manner, she makes "practical" use of a matchbox to play another of her whimsical tricks—holding a violet as a surprise gift for grandmother. On yet another occasion, in a game of "playing ladies,"—children's fantasized interpretation of adult experience, Kezia displays Mrs. Fairfield's love for orderliness in a most precise manner:

The dinner was baking beautifully on a concrete step. She began to lay the cloth on a pink garden seat. In front of each person she put two geranium leaf plates, a pine needle fork and a twig knife. There were three daisy heads on a laurel leaf for poached eggs, some slices of fuchsia petal cold beef, some lovely little rissoles made of earth and water and dandelion seeds, and the chocolate custard which she had decided to serve in the pawa shell she had cooked it in. (43)

Here the make-believe kitchen echoes the granny's world where order reigns and "everything is in pairs" (29).

The duck-beheading scene further illustrates Kezia's terror for disorder which she shares with Mrs. Fairfield. When Pat proceeds to demonstrate "how the kings of Ireland chop the head off a duck" (48), the spurting blood initiates Kezia into both the knowledge of death—a mystery belonging to the adult world, and the awareness of a menace to the established pattern of life. Her violent scream "Put head back! Put head back!" (51) is simultaneously an expression of grief at the loss of a life and a fantasized attempt at, in Daly's term, "the restoration of order" (71).

The reader also finds traces of Linda in Kezia's dream world. The animalistic male sexual threat which repulses Linda assumes the form of the bullying Samuel Josephs' boys in Kezia's consciousness. While Linda, despite all her hatred for Stanley, chooses to accept life's cruelty with a languid resignation, Kezia feigns an indifference in face of the hurts, both real and exaggerated in fantasy, inflicted upon her by the Josephs:

Pooh! She didn't care! A tear rolled down her cheek, but she wasn't crying. She couldn't have cried in front of those awful Samuel Josephs. She sat with her head bent, and as the tear dripped slowly down, she caught it with a neat little whisk of her tongue and ate it before any of them had seen. (5)

As with Linda, Kezia's dream experience also echoes her waking thoughts. Her awareness of the threat of male sexuality, for example, frequently emerges in the form of animals rushing and swelling in her nightmare. "I hate rushing animals," Kezia tells the storeman on her ride to the new house, "I often dream that animals rush at me—even camels—and while they are rushing, their heads swell e— enormous" (10). The similar horror enters Linda's mind in her description of Stanley whom she calls "my Newfoundland dog"; "If only he wouldn't jump at her so, and bark so loudly, and watch her with such eager, loving eyes. He was too strong for her; she had always hated things that rush at her, from a child" (61). Thus, by establishing these associations with Mrs. Fairfield and Linda through the medium of fantasy, Mansfield explores two possibilities for the full growth of Kezia's personality, reflecting and incorporating both her grandmother's practicality and her mother's sensitivity.

M. H. Abrams makes a broad distinction between the method of "telling" and that of "showing" in characterization (21). It is now a commonplace that the shift of emphasis from plot to consciousness, from instruction to revelation, that is, from "telling" to "showing," largely claims Mansfield's innovation in character portrayal. When examining fantasy as a contributive factor to Mansfield's strength in characterization, one should not omit the use of interior monologue which reinforces the "showing" process. Her protagonists' split personalities and the resultant multi-existences are explored in depth through the description of their indulgence in fantasy, as well as through the manner in which this indulgence is conveyed to us. Since the reader does not have to rely upon the narrator as the only source of information, his perspectives are considerably expanded. With the alternative use of authorial voice and interior monologue, Mansfield is able to examine her subject both from a distance and within a close range, and to bridge the interior and exterior views by slipping in and out of her characters' fantasy world. As the reader is given an opportunity to compare the difference between the two views, the characterization is accomplished with relative objectivity.

An illustrative example of the apt use of interior monologue can be found in "The Little Governess." Through the long passages recording the governess' reveries in the train, the author achieves two ends simultaneously: the revelation of her heroine's fantasized vision of life, the internal cause of her tragic experience in Munich, and the exposure of the sinister forces operating in the objective reality which is erroneously reflected in her consciousness. Beryl Fairfield's narcissistic meditation in front of the looking glass, likewise, functions to link the two worlds—a subjective world of possibilities and an objective world of fixity.

This function of the interior monologue also exhibits itself in Mansfield's other stories. In "The Voyage," for instance, Fenella's silent observation frequently interrupts the authorial description of the travelling scene, thus unfolding the little heroine's wandering existence between a transparent childhood and an unpredictable world of adult reality. In "The Daughters of the Late Colonel," towards the end of the narrative, the reader finds Constantia standing before her favorite Buddha in her dead father's room, thinking loud: "What did it mean? What was it she was always wanting? What did it all lead to? Now? Now" (*The Garden Party and Other Stories* 127)? Her wondering thought betrays her desperate albeit vain attempt to coordinate and unify her dream of personal fulfillment and the reality of filial obligations. In these interconnective moments, the characters become thematically as well as philosophically true, for they convey "the total pattern" of "a dichotomy—the irreconcilable cleavage between the rich potentialities of life and the inescapable brutalities of human experience which must evoke despair." (Berkman 159)

CHAPTER III

FANTASY: IMAGERY AND SYMBOLISM

Many critics have noticed Katherine Mansfield's affinity with the French symbolists, especially her adherence to the Symbolist theory in her artistic practice. The essence of this theory, Clare Hanson and Andrew Gurr believe, is to "convey abstract states of mind or feeling only through concrete images, which act as 'objective correlatives' for them" (50). As early as 1908, in an annotation of Arthur Symons' *Studies in Prose and Verse*, Mansfield has declared her rejection of analytical description and her preference for a revelation through suggestive "gestures:"

> The partisans of analysis describe minutely the state of the soul; the secret motive of every action as being of far greater importance than the action itself. The partisans of objectivity—give us the result of this evolution sans describing the secret processes. They evoke the state of soul through the slightest gesture—i.e. realize flesh covered bones—which is the artists method for me – in as much as art seems to me **pure vision** –I am indeed a partisan of objectivity. (*The Critical Writings of Katherine Mansfield* 140)

Mansfield's literary creation confirms that she has worked assiduously towards "this art of exclusion and suggestion" (Hanson and Gurr 50). An examination of her writing career reveals that she reaches her artistic peak when in her works the analysis of motives completely gives way to a series of carefully arranged images. The significance of these images is two-fold: symbolically, they represent the unfulfilled dream or fantasy of her characters; thematically, they constitute a part of the reality in which they exist. As a general rule, the narrative is successful when its imagery pattern satisfies both the symbolic and thematic needs. In stories where images are disconnected from thematic function, the symbolism towards which they work is usually unnatural and forced. The aloe tree establishes itself as an effective central image in "Prelude" exactly because of its fulfillment of the dual functions. It not only suggests Linda's secret aspiration for freedom from sexual bondage but also helps to shape the Burnells' new domestic setting, an element crucial to the characters' changing moods. The elegant black hat in "The Garden Party" is employed, likewise, both to heighten the atmosphere of the party as the theme requires and to symbolize the female vanity of the moneyed class, a major component of the Sheridans' fantasy world.

However, not every story in Mansfield's canon enjoys an equal degree of success in this regard. "Mr. and Mrs. Dove," for example, is obviously one of her failures. Mansfield endeavors, in this story, to draw a parallel between the dove's bowing in pursuit of his mate and the young hero Reginald's persistent quest for his true love. But the effect of this parallel and its attendant symbolic implication are seriously impaired because of the lack of an inherent connection to the basic narrative theme. "The Fly" is another example where the power of symbolism is weakened as the central image, the fly, fails to fit closely into the thematic context. The rich suggestiveness found elsewhere is largely missing, because the equation between the fate of the insect and that of human beings "has a simplicity which verges on the crude" (Hanson and Gurr 130).

To Mansfield, the maturing process of art is also a process in which the image pattern moves towards variety and complexity. This process is a painful, spiral-shaped one. John Middleton Murry has endeavored to summarize it in four distinctive stages, each bearing the mark of her emotional experience:

(1) a sort of bitter revulsion from life—which is characteristic of her work prior to **Prelude**;

(2) a joyous and loving acceptance of life—which finds its first complete expression in **Prelude**;

(3) then a far more poignant disillusion with and revulsion from life – "**nessun**

maggior dolore"—which found its first complete expression in **Bliss**, and gradually deepened through experience into the very profound sense of hopelessness which finds expression in **Je ne parle pas**; and, finally,

(4) an acceptance even of this hopelessness: and out of this acceptance comes the last perfection of her work. (*Katherine Mansfield and Other Literary Studies* 88)

Unfortunately, later critics have fallen too much under the sway of Murry's judgment, which tends to see Mansfield's artistic achievement in rigidly divided chronological periods rather than as a coherent unity. A survey of her works shows that her writing does not fall exactly into Murry's classification. For example, Linda and Beryl in "Prelude," a story composed in a state of "joyous and loving acceptance of life" according to Murry, are evidently tinged with a sadness bordering upon despair over their bootless attempt to escape the trap of daily existence. They are, therefore, as tragic and helpless as Mansfield's later heroines. On the other hand, in "The Fly" and "The Life of Ma Parker," written only a few months before her death, an undisguised outcry against the misery of human condition can be clearly heard. Life's bitterness has not yet tamed her protagonists into a state of complete resignation as Murry would have us believe. However, Murry's singling out of "Prelude" as a watershed in Mansfield's artistic career is both justifiable and perceptive.

In Mansfield's early stories prior to "Prelude" (including her juvenilia), the images contributing to her characters' fantasy world are relatively unvaried and fixed. They frequently assume the form of a human figure embodying the unfulfilled desires in life: a loving parent or a lover and soul-mate. The dream figure is either a pure creation of fantasy, like the tender snow-white lady in "His Ideal" and the mysterious and elusive woodswoman in "My Potplant," or a real personality transformed into a half-fairy figure through the characters' imagination, like the talented musician David in "Juliet" and the "god grandfather" in "The Little Governess."

In these early experimental pieces, Mansfield's protagonists are allowed very limited space to move, for they breathe only in their compartmentalized life of fantasy. Their world of fantasy, furthermore, eddies almost exclusively around their real or imaginary contacts with these dream figures. Very representative of works under this category is "Something Childish but Very Natural," written in 1913 but published posthumously in 1924, a story Cherry Hankin describes as "the first encounter of youthful dream with adult reality" (*Confessional Stories* 97).

The story opens with a chance meeting of two youngsters, Henry and Edna, on a commuting train to London. Immediately striking the reader is Mansfield's use of imagery which conveys Henry's indulgence in day-dreaming. Charmed by a little poem, "Something Childish but Very Natural," because "it's got a smile of a dream on it" (*Something Childish and Other Stories* 130), he nearly misses the train, an incident which leads to his acquaintance with Edna. He is presented to us as a youth who gets bored early in life by "all the dull horrid things" (139) and attributes this boredom to the pressure of society. "It's people that make things so—silly," he declares, "as long as you can keep away from them you're safe and you're happy" (140). In Edna, he soon finds alliance because her dreamy presence provides him with a sense of escape from the men-packed society.

Mansfield employs images that depict Edna as strange and mysterious. Everything about her seems veiled. Her face and shoulder are only half visible because of the cascade of hair; her hands are hidden from the sight in gloves; and even her voice sounds vague and remote. When Henry finally obtains a glimpse of her raised face, her grey eyes are still covered "under the shadow of her hat" and her lips only "faintly parted" (132). This half-human, half-elf creature soon expands to monopolize Henry's fantasy world. Her dreamy presence makes his heart swell "bigger and bigger and trembling like a marvelous bubble—so that he is afraid to breathe for fear of breaking it" (133). As a result, his contact with the throbbing real life diminishes to its minimum:

> He tried to remember what it had felt like without Edna, but he could not get back
> to those days. They were hidden by her; Edna, with the marigold hair and strange,

dreamy smile filled him up to the brim. He breathed her; he ate and drank her. He walked about with a shining ring of Edna keeping the world away or touching whatever it lighted on with its own beauty. (151)

The images Mansfield adopts continue to point to Edna's mysteriousness as the theme complicates. In their second meeting, the reader finds her suddenly descending into Henry's presence as if from a fairyland where "white smoke floated… dissolved and came again in swaying wreaths" (135). She listens with "a dreamy smile" (147) to Henry's description of their prospective Utopian home. Most indicative of her ethereal qualities is her shrinking from any physical contacts with her lover. Half indulging in and half frightened by this elusiveness of hers, Henry needs physical intimacy to eliminate the distance between them. "He wanted to kiss Edna, and to put his arms around her and press her to him and feel her cheek hot against his kiss and kiss her until he'd no breath left and so stifle the dream" (152). His ambivalence contributes to the major irony of the story: the one whose existence largely leans upon fantasy should feel so insecure in his own dream world.

In Mansfield's juvenilia including "His Ideal" and "Juliet," death is frequently called upon to fuse the gap between fantasy and reality, where her characters can dwell in eternity with their dream figures. But in "Something Childish," dream, the state of near-death, ironically brings her protagonist closer to reality. In Henry's waking experience, Edna fulfills his vision of ideal human relationship through her ultimate consent to his physical intimacy and even his plan for "playing house"— a fantasized Utopian kingdom of love. Yet in his dream, she betrays his faith by transforming herself, first into a white flying moth, then into a treacherous little girl with a telegram in her hand. This irreconcilability between "demands of fantasy" and "real life needs," as Hankin points out, determines the inevitability of the story's ending:

He (Henry) and Edna have come together precisely because they believe themselves to be quite different from ordinary people. Since the make-believe existence they build is based on this premise, any move towards accepting themselves as normal human beings is bound to threaten, if not destroy, their relationship. (*Confessional Stories* 88)

This story, together with Mansfield's other early experimental pieces in symbolism, is obviously immature. Despite her preference for a revelation of the state of soul through concrete and suggestive images, the symbolic implication underlying the narrative is conveyed through a distanced, abstracted and almost emblematic human figure. Edna's sole occupancy of Henry's social horizon blocks the interaction between the realms of fantasy and reality, thus transfiguring the story's setting into that of a semi-fairytale.

This emblematic presentation of a "dream figure" as the center of symbolism gradually disappears as Mansfield matures. Stories published since "Prelude" witness an evident change in image patterns. To explore the interrelation between fantasy and mimesis, Mansfield starts to look for her images and metaphors not in a single conceptualized dream figure but in a vast natural world. Her letters and journals of this period are overflowing with warm feelings towards nature. "It is as though the mechanized and militarized world in which she lived did not exist in any fundamental way in her imagination" (Zinman 458). Here "imagination" can be readily substituted for "fantasy." This rich variety of imagery found in the natural world points towards, with their variety and vitality, the unlimited possibilities for life in human imagination as against the barrenness and fixity of reality. "Bliss," composed shortly after the publication of "Prelude," is one of the first stories which evinces this progress.

It is noteworthy that "Bliss" is completed only a few days after Mansfield's first hemorrhage. The terror of this fatal illness is redoubled as she has to bear the shock alone in France where she was stranded by the raging war. This shock, however, strangely agitates her passionate love for life and eager appreciation of the beauty of nature. She reports to Murry this state of mind in a letter dated February 20, 1918, the second day after the consumptive attack:

> Since this little attack I've had, a queer thing has happened. I feel that my love and longing for the external world—I mean the world of nature—has suddenly increased a million times. When I think of the little flowers that grow in grass, and little streams and places where we can lie and look up at the clouds—Oh, I simply ache for them—for them with you. (*Letters to Murry* 175)

As Sylvia Berkman indicates, it is not by accident that this mood "is related to the essential theme of 'Bliss'—the immutability of natural beauty in the face of human disaster" (107). This theme is executed through a series of images the author constructs around her characters, Bertha Young in particular.

Marvin Magalaner, in "Traces of Her 'Self' in Katherine Mansfield's 'Bliss'," ascribes Bertha's "graph of... emotions" which "moves from the heights of joyous exhilaration (bliss) to the depths of despair" to a train of discoveries she makes during the brief span of an afternoon and evening. One of these discoveries, Magalaner argues, is her husband's "infidelity in the suddenly grasped relationship" with Pearl Fulton. The reader also shares the new knowledge that

> Bertha's mystical relationship [with Pearl] cannot be regained; that Bertha's relationship to her own child is less firm than the child's ties to her nurse; that Bertha's position as hostess to a bizarre group of bohemian pseudo-intellectuals does not qualify her to enter into communion with them, or them with her. (414)

However, Magalaner fails to perceive a fundamental discovery which leads to and accounts for all others: the discrepancy between supposition and fact, or imagination and truth. This discovery, the main thread of the thematic structure, is related to the reader primarily through a changing pattern of imagery connecting the story's protagonist and her surroundings.

Mansfield discloses the narrative by presenting Bertha in a deceptive fantasy world through her immediate association with the sun. Bertha's first entrance into the story is accompanied with an almost hysterical display of emotion which she imagines to be "bliss":

> What can you do if you are thirty and, turning the corner of your own street, you are overcome, suddenly, by a feeling of bliss—absolute bliss!—as though you'd suddenly swallowed a bright piece of that late afternoon sun and it burned in your bosom, sending out a little shower of sparks into every particle, into every finger and toe? (*Bliss and Other stories* 116)

Bertha's kinship to the sun is made more overt when fantasy dominates her mood. In daily life, she finds herself "so cold" (133) and her body "shut up in a case like a rare, rare fiddle" (116). When indulging in fantasy, she feels her heart expanded with passion and desire which burns from within. Thus the afore-quoted sun metaphor is sustained.

It is this burning desire that motivates her strange behavior of arranging the fruits for the evening party into "two pyramids of... bright round" breast shapes (118), and her sudden impulse to hug the cushion in the drawing-room "passionately, passionately" (122). Both of the two actions, the fantasized gesture for sexual fulfillment, prove to be ineffectual, for they cannot "put out the fire in her bosom," causing instead "the contrary" (122). Bertha's passion is dubious and complicated, for it involves both an explicit sexual longing for her husband Harry Young and an implicit desire for Pearl Fulton, a new "find" of hers with whom she declares to be "in love" (121).

Through a contrastive moon image which Pearl embodies, Bertha's connection with the sun in the fantasy scenes is further established. Judith S. Neaman has drawn our attention to Pearl's unmistakable "lunar qualities" as a foil to Bertha's solar warmth (244). However, her attempt to trace the motif of the story to the biblical source sounds far-fetched. Pearl is introduced into the scene in a moonlit evening, dressed "all in silver, with a silver fillet binding her pale blond hair" (127). When she sits at Harry's side turning a tangerine, her slender fingers are "so pale" that a "light seems to come from them" (129–30). Like the moon, she is aloof and treacherous.

She seldom looks at people "directly;" her eyelids are "heavy" and her smile "strange" and incomplete (128). More suggestive of her penchant for secretiveness is her vague and remote voice which constantly murmurs and intimates, creating ambiguity rather than clarity, misunderstanding instead of communication. But in an over-emotionalized state, Bertha allows herself to blur the demarcation between imagination and fact, fantasy and existence. She insists on interpreting Pearl's equivocation as "signals" for a willingness to communicate, although her confidence is at times punctuated with doubt and confusion:

> What she simply couldn't make out—what was miraculous—was how she should have guessed Miss Fulton's mood so exactly and so instantly. For she never doubted for a moment that she was right, and yet what had she to go on? **Less than nothing** [emphasis mine]. (130)

Bertha is confused not only by Pearl's elusive lunar qualities, but also by the multiplicity of other associations around her which allow for many possible interpretations. Pearl is also connected, for instance, with the grey cat creeping across the lawn with its dragging shadow, which Kate Fullbrook reads as an indication of her sexuality as "both transcendent and utterly sordid" (101–02). The polarity of images and their associative implications combine to establish the duality of Pearl's existence and, therefore, the inevitability of the crush of Bertha's fantasy world. Fullbrook summarizes this technique admiringly as the one in which "symbols are selected and placed with great tact and evocativeness, suggesting their meanings without ever insisting on them" (101).

Mansfield's maturing treatment of symbolism in "Bliss" also exhibits itself in the manner with which she harmonizes the polarized images. Bertha and Pearl, for examples, are depicted as two opposites: one with the sun-like emotional candescence and candidness, the other possessing the moon's coolness, remoteness and mystery. Yet they are unified in their common attachment to the pear tree which grows in Bertha's garden.

The tree's symbolic implication has roused a great deal of critical debate. Some critics, including Chester Eisinger, emphasize the tree's phallic quality, and connecting it, therefore, with Harry, whom both Bertha and Pearl covet (Item 48). Others, of whom Walter E. Anderson is one, regard it as "a composite symbol representing in its tallness Bertha's homosexual aspirations and in its full, rich blossoms, her desire to be sexually used" (400). Its flowers, Anderson further argues, are "her female sexual self" whereas its "tall assertiveness" symbolizes the "masculine part of her sexual feelings" which yet "eludes her conscious recognition" (400). Both of the above propositions need some qualification, as the former fails to explain the tree's state of blossoming, an evidence of its femininity; whereas, the latter does not extend the symbolism to include Pearl, with whom homosexuality has no obvious association. A more natural and logic connection has to be established following the development of the theme. The tree, we notice, is ushered into the scene when Bertha is standing by the drawing-room window overlooking the garden, brimming with the feeling of "bliss":

> At the far end, against the wall, there was a tall, slender pear tree in fullest, richest bloom; it stood perfect, as though becalmed against the jade-green sky. Bertha couldn't help feeling, even from this distance, that it had not a single bud or a faded petal. (122)

It is obvious that Bertha is mesmerized by the tree's primeness of life. There is no wasted youth nor fading old age, for all the flowers are fully open, suggestive of Bertha's mature womanhood. As if afraid of losing the grasp of its evanescent essence by tarrying, Bertha hastily claims "this lovely pear tree" as "a symbol of her own life" (123).

From the outset, Bertha's life, just like the blossoming pear tree, is perfect and fruitful—social prestige, material affluence and accessibility to fashion, cultural charms and friendship. Also seeming to resemble this productive yet "becalmed" tree is the love between the Youngs, which, though beyond the stage of violent emotional turbulence, is mature and steady, as Bertha believes. Yet underneath this beautiful fantasy of perfection, there stand shadows against which she wants to shut her eyes; just like under the vivacious pear blossoms, there is the ugly cat, the sight of which gives her "a curious shiver" (122). The tree is, therefore, more closely related to Bertha's fantasized vision of what life should be. Immediately threatening this vision of bliss is the gloomy presence of unfulfilled wishes. What she chooses in face of the "creepy" sight of reality is to turn "away from the window" and begin "walking up and down" (123).

The tree's association with fantasy is extended, as the theme develops, to include Pearl. When Pearl suggests, towards the end of the story, to view the garden, Bertha's heart quivers with excitement at this "sign" of communication:

> And the two women stood there side by side looking at the slender, flowering tree. Although it was so still it seemed, like the flame of a candle, to stretch up, to point, to quiver in the bright air, to grow taller and taller as they gazed—almost to touch the rim of the round, silver moon. (131)

Here the polarized qualities of the two women, the solar warmth and lunar serenity, find themselves harmonized in the image of the pear tree. This is a rare moment of sharing, as both of them experience a state of abeyance of self in their common dream about life's unlimited potentiality:

> How long did they stand there? Both, as it were, caught in that circle of unearthly light, understanding each other perfectly, creatures of another world, and wondering what they were to do in this one with all this blissful treasure that burned in their bosoms and dropped, in silver flowers, from their hair and hands? (131)

The tree's unearthly qualities heighten its symbolic effect that Mansfield intends to create. Its inaccessibility corresponds to the illusive nature of the two women's dream—its blossoming youth and vitality, together with their dream of life's perfectibility, all belong to quite "another world." By establishing the parallel between the tree and the characters' aspirations, Mansfield reveals another controversial aspect of human fate—an unquenchable desire for truth and love in human relationships mingled with an inevitable despair over the unattainability of them.

The correspondence between the remoteness of the images and the elusiveness of their implications is also found elsewhere in the story. Our realization that Bertha's vision of sexual fulfillment with her husband and spiritual union with Pearl is doomed to destruction comes together with our knowledge of the inaccessibility of the sun, with which she is unmistakably associated. Pearl's moon-like aloofness is, nevertheless, undercut by her base relationship with Harry. Some of the critics, such as Neaman (246) and Magalaner ("Traces of Her 'Self'" 415), have noticed the connection between the libido for food and the excessive sexual appetite in many of Mansfield's male characters, including Harry, but few of them see the recurrent food images in "Bliss" as a sharp contrast to the soaring images which surround the presence of Bertha and Pearl. Harry's vocabulary, for example, is riddled with phrases alluding to animal organs and alimentary function of human body. Among the most frequently used terms in his description and assessment of values are "a good stomach," "liver frozen," "pure flatulence" or "kidney disease" (122). At the dinner party, in particular, his conversation about food adds another shade to the sexual innuendo:

> Harry was enjoying his dinner. It was part of his—well, not his nature, exactly, and certainly not his pose—his—something or other—to talk about food and the glory in his "shameless passion for the white flesh of the lobster" and "the green of pistachio ices—green and cold like the eyelids of Egyptian dancers." (129)

The habit of elucidating thoughts through expressions related to food is also discovered in those who come to associate with Harry, namely, his bohemian friends. When Mrs. Norman Knight, alias Face, talks about decorating a room for the Jacob Nathans, her design is based upon "a fried-fish scheme, with the backs of the chairs shaped like frying pans and lovely chip potatoes embroidered all over the curtains" (132). During the dinner, Eddie Warren, another of Harry's invitees, cites works entitled "Stomach Trouble" (129) and "Table d'Hote," beginning with "Why

Must it Always be Tomato Soup" (135)? Like Bertha's sun and Pearl's moon, their affinity to food images also betrays part of their personality—greedy, pretentious, and lacking the fundamental power for imagination. While Bertha and Pearl are bestowed with the celestial qualities which enable them to soar in the spiritual realm of fantasy, Harry and his friends, in their excessive love for vulgar pleasures, are doomed to be earthbound as "creatures of this world."

In Mansfield's later works, especially those completed during the last years of her life, the presentation of symbolism demonstrates a conceivable departure from what we have perceived in "Prelude" and "Bliss." There is a tendency to return to the concentration of images; and the fantasy world in which her characters reside is again portrayed through single symbolically suggestive images. In "The Fly", for instance, the pitiful little insect struggling for life constitutes the story's central symbolism, although its function has stirred a good deal of critical controversy. The fly shapes the focal point of the hero's fantasy world, and indeed, the only possibility by which he can "dream about alternativeness"—an exchange of position with the omnipotent divine power. By placing in a parallel, though much too obvious, the death of a son and the death of a fly, Mansfield "invites us to make a metaphysical equation between the boss as he toys with the life of the fly, and God or the gods, playing with the lives of human beings 'for their sport'" (Hanson and Gurr 130). This reliance upon single symbolic imagery is again found in "The Life of Ma Parker." The memories of her dead grandson Lennie offer the haggard charwoman the only opportunity to indulge in her dream world where the present ceases to exist and hurt.

One of the representative examples of the last phase in Mansfield's creative life is "The Doll's House," a story, along with "The Garden Party" and "Ma Parker," which Paul Delany calls "short and simple annals of the poor" (7) in a phrase borrowed from Gray's "Elegy." The central and indeed the only vehicle for symbolism of the story is the doll's house, around which the narrative climax is built. The house, a present for the Burnell children from Mrs. Hay, excites two levels of narrative interest. It is, primarily, a symbol of wealth and class distinction to the Burnell girls, not even excluding the sensitive and sympathetic Kezia. It functions, at the same time, as an embodiment of a childhood fantasy for all the girls who come to view it.

The possession of the doll's house is "both physical and imaginative" (Maxwell-Mahon 48) to Isabel, the first daughter of the Burnell family. When the house first arrives, what immediately catches the children's, especially Isabel's eyes is its elegance which parallels their own residence. To Isabel, the house is both a part of her childhood reality and a part of her childhood fantasy. It enables her to play two roles simultaneously—the real role of an eldest girl who has the natural claim of priority to the doll's house; and the imaginative role of "the lady of the house" who possesses and guards her own properties with a sense of complacency typical of the moneyed class:

> They [the Burnell girls] burned to tell everybody, to describe, to—well—to boast about their doll's house before the school-bell rang.
>
> "I'm to tell," said Isabel, "because I'm the eldest. And you two can join in after. But I'm to tell first."
>
> There was nothing to answer. Isabel was bossy, but she was always right, and Lottie and Kezia knew too well the powers that went with being eldest. They brushed through the thick buttercups at the road edge and said nothing.
>
> "And I'm to choose who's to come and see it first. Mother said I might." (3–4)

Obviously, Isabel's love for hierarchic order is but an extension of the philosophy of the adult world where wealth and seniority count. Just as the possession of the doll's house is actual and concrete, so the dream about the future power for the first Burnell princess is tangible, needing only time to come true. The house serves, therefore, not only as an imitative version of the Burnell estate with all its material splendor, but also as a fantasized world in which the snob-in-the-making prepares herself for a formal take-over of the power of adult snobs.

The material aspect of the doll's house, which appeals to Isabel as its essential quality, loses much of its charm in the eyes of Kezia, the underprivileged third daughter of the Burnells. To her "the father and mother dolls" look "very stiff as though they had fainted in the drawing-room" (3). This vividly reflects the moral rigidity and lack of genuine affection of the real Burnell parental figures. Kezia's observation that the children dolls are "really too big for the doll's house" (3) reveals, furthermore, her awareness of her own state in the family—outgrown in and stifled by an environment that is spiritually confining. What generates her real excitement about the doll's house is the little lamp in the kitchen:

> ... What Kezia liked more than anything, what she liked frightfully, was the lamp. It stood in the middle of the dining room table, an exquisite little amber lamp with a white globe. It was even filled all ready for lighting, though, of course, you couldn't light it. But there was something inside that looked like oil and moved when you shook it. (3)

Kezia's reason for loving the lamp seems simple at first sight. The lamp to her is "perfect," "real" and fitting (3) as compared to the dolls who are unnatural and out of place. Yet ironically, the dolls' artificiality reflects her true state of existence whereas the little lamp, the most "real" item in the false surrounding, points towards her world of fantasy.

Unlike the image patterns that appear in Mansfield's early works, the interpretations of which are relatively limited and fixed, the lamp in "The Doll's House" invites a rich variety of possible connotative associations. Hanson and Gurr's definition of the lamp as a symbol of "art," "the central reality amidst the material splendours of the doll's house" (128) sounds a little out of focus for two reasons. First, the main theme of the story is woven around an intuitive, rather than intellectual, understanding of life. Secondly, the lamp is the only item in the house which possesses the capability of inspiring dreams about changes while all the rest is irretrievably fixed. Delany's explanation of the lamp as an epitome, for Kezia in particular, of "those qualities of warmth, brightness, and security that make a house into a home" (12) is more apt to the theme of the narrative. The juxtaposition of the stiff dolls and the vivacious lamp illustrates Mansfield's attempt at polarizing the rigidity of the bourgeois morality which centers on material values and the possibility of a genuine love and warmth in human relationships.

It is quite obvious that the Burnell estate is more a house than a home to Kezia, and her sense of oppression originates from two sources—the tyrannical ruling of her parents and the self-willed dominance of her eldest sister. At home, Kezia is less favoured and her voice not heard. To the adult Burnells, the desire to share feelings with their children is minimal, as parental duty is only a rough equation of material provision. When Kezia ventures to ask for permission to invite the outcast Kelvey girls, her first move towards communication with her mother is sharply dismissed. This sense of oppression is also extended to Kezia's life in school where Isabel almost always outshines her. When Isabel proudly details the marvels of the interior of the doll's house, Kezia's claim that "the lamp's the best of all" is generally ignored (7). Kezia's position in the family parallels that of the Kelvey sisters' in the social edifice, and it is only natural that they share her feelings about the lamp.

The lamp, with its power to illuminate and transform darkness, symbolizes simultaneously Kezia's awakening to the knowledge of the cruelty of life and her imaginative power that transcends and recreates reality. If the whole setting of the doll's house is the miniature form of the adult society where hypocrisy and snobbery prevail, the lamp stands alone guarding the sovereignty of a childhood fantasy where truth and beauty reign. The lamp's metaphoric implication as a child's dream vision of life against the adult insanity is also found in "Prelude." It is no coincidence that Aunt Beryl hates to see Kezia connected with the lamp in both of the stories. In "The Doll's House," she rudely interrupts Kezia's introduction of the beauty of the lamp by driving away her only audience, the Kelveys. In "Prelude," she almost snatches the lamp away from Kezia's hands the night when they arrive in their new home. Like the lamp, which, despite all its attractions, cannot be lit for practical use, Kezia's fantasy is not likely to survive the cruel force of adult reality.

The lamp also indicates the fantasy world of the Kelvey sisters, Lil and Else, although the dream of the washerwoman's daughters is of quite another nature. If Kezia suffers only from indifference both at home and in school, the Kelveys are openly taunted and despised everywhere they set their feet. Yet the Kelveys are able to stand this social banishment with an aloofness bordering upon ostrichism. They are portrayed as two of the rare girls in school who possess a capability to dream, which protect them from being hurt by the malicious force of social discrimination. Their innate imaginative power is first revealed through their ardent love for nature, although they can only afford the "dreadfully common-looking flowers" to their teacher. Another evidence of that power is the sisters' intuitive understanding of each other without even the aid of language:

> She [Else] scarcely ever spoke. She went through life holding on to Lil, with a piece of Lil's skirt screwed up in her hand. Where Lil went, our Else followed. In the playground, on the road going to and from school, there was Lil marching in front and our Else holding on behind. Only when she wanted anything, or when she was out of breath, our Else gave Lil a tug, a twitch, and Lil stopped and turned round. The Kelveys never failed to understand each other. (6)

This imaginative power immediately draws them to Kezia's comment on the lamp, while all the other girls are fascinated by Isabel's account of the sensational carpet. At the end of the narrative, Else shows that Kezia's point has registered. It is this great appeal of the lamp that overcomes their fear and finally leads them to the Burnells' courtyard. In the last scene of the story, Mansfield's preference for the Kelveys becomes evident, for the moment of epiphany is unfolded in Else's climactic cry, the only opportunity when we hear her speak:

> … Dreamily they looked over the hay paddocks, past the creek, to the group of wattles where Logan's cows stood waiting to be milked. What were their thoughts?
> Presently our Else nudged up close to her sister. But now she had forgotten the cross lady [Beryl]. She put out a finger and stroked her sister's quill; she smiled her rare smile.
> "I seen the little lamp," she said, softly.
> Then both were silent once more. (12–13)

This ability to appreciate life's transcendent beauty in face of the ugliness and cruelty of daily existence ranks the Kelveys mentally superior to the vulgar school girls. Kezia's alliance with them also opens a possibility of human understanding and communication across the gulf of social ranks. Kezia and the Kelveys' "dream about alternatives" through their attachment to the little lamp merges into Mansfield's main stream of symbolic use of images—they all "function as protests against any ideology of fixture and certainty" (Fullbrook 128).

Thus, from "His Ideal" to "The Doll's House," we witness a complete circle of development in Mansfield's use of imagery. As Mansfield has always regarded art as "pure vision," this gradual development as found in her works corresponds to the expansion of her vision of life. In the early experimental stage, her understanding of life is restricted to a narrow interpretation of events and situations personally concerning her, and her fantasy world is much too attached to her autobiographical experiences to reflect universal truth. The images with which she constructs the world of vision, usually in the form of a dream figure, are relatively fixed because of a lack of rich suggestiveness. Neither the surrogate mother figure nor the ideal soul-mates, as in "His Ideal," "Juliet," and "Something Childish," leave a lasting impression on the reader, because they fail to present the possibility of alternatives essential to human dreams.

Yet her fatal disease and the raging world war soon enable Mansfield to see her own suffering in the light of general human fate. Her fantasy world starts to shift from the pure personal to the more universal, and the imagery pattern makes corresponding move towards variety and complexity. Works composed during this period, particularly "Prelude" and "Bliss," though still confessional, are able to reflect an expanded view of life through a series of more suggestive images. Bertha's anguish in "Bliss," for example, stems from an individual as well as a universal desire for understanding and love. The diversity of images which connect the heroine's dream world and reality, the sun, the moon, and the pear tree, reveals the unlimited potentiality in human imagination for changes.

This profound understanding of life, or "burning gaze" in Elizabeth Bowen's term, does not last long, for "vision at full intensity is not by nature to be sustained; it is all but bound to be intermittent" (89–90). This explains, perhaps, the uneven quality in the works completed in the last stage of Mansfield's artistic career. We have, among her masterpieces, "The Doll's House" and "The Garden Party," in which the selection of the images accommodates the demands of both fantasy and real life. At the same time, we also find some less successful examples, including "The Fly." In her desperate attempt to accomplish her swan song and in her excessive concern about the symbolic significance, Mansfield ignores the organic connection between the images and the narrative context upon which they depend for existence. The fantasy world, therefore, lacks contact with that of reality.

CHAPTER IV

FANTASY AND NARRATIVE STRUCTURE

Katherine Mansfield's narrative structure has been generally regarded as her major claim to modernity. Despite the innovations she brings to it, the essential elements constituting a conventional narrative structure are still present in her works. The recurrent use of fantasy plays an important part in both her departure from and her adherence to the traditional concept of narrative structure.

The accusations of critics cited by A. L. Bader in his article on the structure of modern short stories in general reflect, perhaps, how some of the reader must have felt about Mansfield's works in particular:

> They maintain that the modern short story is plotless, static, fragmentary, amorphous—frequently a mere character sketch or vignette, or a mere reporting of a transient moment, or the capturing of a mood or nuance—everything, in fact, except a story. (40)

Bader proceeds to defend the modern story writers by showing the presence, in their works, of three elements essential to the formation of narrative structure: progression of plot, or in other words, conflict; climax issuing from the conflict; and finally, a resolution (40). However, this basic pattern, Bader believes, is capable of "considerable variation", for

> plot is not necessarily a strait jacket, as in the formula story, and it is only one of the elements of complete short-story form. Hence plot may be the dominant element in a story, or again it may be subordinated to elements such as character, theme, or atmosphere. Conflict may be of two fundamental types: external conflict, in which a character struggles against a tangible obstacle, and internal conflict, or conflict within a

character. Also, there are wide differences as to how soon the conflict is made apparent to the reader and how much of it he is allowed to understand early in the story. (41)

"The modern short story," Bader concludes, "demonstrates its claim to the possession of narrative structure derived from plot" despite its technical variations (45). The key feature underlying these variations is the method of "indirection" (43)—indirection in introducing plot progression, conflict, and the ultimate resolution.

Bader's forceful vindication of the art of the modern short story can be roughly applied to the assessment of Mansfield's narrative structure. Mansfield's works have attracted criticism as possessing "neither **beginning** nor **end**, "for she starts "with a **plop**, as the human situation drops into the reader's consciousness" and then "withdraws herself entirely" without bothering about a solution (Ward 286). Criticism of this sort has obviously confused the basic elements which constitute the narrative structure with the techniques which make them manifest. A selective reading from her canon will help us to discover the evolution of a structural pattern which, reinforced by fantasy scenes, bears out Bader's theory of "indirection."

As the primary element of narrative structure, plot in Mansfield's stories demonstrates a conceivable departure from its conventional meaning. E. M. Forster in *Aspects of the Novel* defines plot as "a narrative of events" arranged in "time-sequence" with an emphasis on "causality" (93). Robert Scholes and Robert Kellogg, on the other hand, consider plot as "the dynamic, sequential element in narrative." "Insofar as character, or any other element in narrative literature," they further argue, "becomes dynamic, it is a part of the plot" (207). Whatever their difference, all of them acknowledge two factors as essential to the formation of plot—progression of action and time-sequence. Yet in Mansfield's fiction, with the entrance of fantasy, plot is shifted from the external world of physical action to the realm of subjectivity, and the narrative action may consist of only a series of mental processes. As a result, the concept about time, which contains and reflects the action, has also changed. While a relative duration, organized in logical sequences, is required for the completion of a physical action in traditional stories, a mental process in Mansfield's works, which possibly transcends the spatial and sequential bounds, takes only some flickering moments.

Regardless of this seeming departure from convention, one of the basic features of plot, namely, the progression of narrative action, is still preserved, though presented in a less direct manner with the shifting of time and space. "Miss Brill" is a very illuminative instance of Mansfield's innovative rendering of plot. The only "action" of which the reader is informed is an aging spinster's walking to and from a public park and her handling of a fur piece. It is obvious that Mansfield's effort to elaborate on these details is minimal. The major portion of the narrative where "action" should have reigned is devoted, contrary to the expectation of a traditional reading public, to the heroine's fantasized vision of her own attraction and importance in social gatherings. The plot, no longer relying upon the progression and the eventual completion of a physical action as tradition demands, is developed in a full circle of mental activities from the height of expectation to the depth of disillusionment. This circle starts with the heroine's exultant albeit illusive feeling as "an actress" on the huge stage of life (*The Garden Party and Other Stories* 204–05) and ends in her painful discovery that she is but a "stupid old thing" in the world of youth (206).

In Mansfield's stories, fantasy also plays a crucial part in the build-up of conflict, the second component of narrative structure according to Bader. Since plot has been shifted, by the intervention of fantasy, from the objective world of physical action to the subjective realm of mental process, the narrative conflict is developed through a few suggestive details, but primarily through the protagonists' introspections. As most of her characters are not "action"-oriented, the battle with life has to be fought in the narrow confines of the human psyche. Yet this internalization does not change the nature of the narrative conflict, that is, the universal discrepancy between soaring human ambition and sordid reality, though now addressed more indirectly through fantasy scenes.

Mansfield's narrative starts, as a general rule, with a seemingly peaceful coexistence of the realms of reality and fantasy. The balance is gradually tilted as the world of reality begins to impinge upon that of fantasy. The narrative reaches its climax when the two come to an open confrontation. A great number of her stories, especially those dealing with the subject of initiation, closely follows this structural pattern. "Her First Ball," a thinly disguised adaptation of the author's adolescent experience, falls exactly into this category. As the story unfolds, the dream of ever-lasting youth and beauty, represented by Leila, the country cousin of the Sheridans, and the reality of life's transience, embodied by the "shabby" "old" man (*The Garden Party and Other Stories* 216), develop as two parallel but separate lines. The inevitability of their clash is indicated, metaphorically, through the meeting between Leila and the man as dancing partners. "You can't hope to last anything like as long as that," he tells her during the dance, "no-o, long before that you'll be sitting up there on the stage, looking on, in your nice black velvet. And these pretty arms will have turned into little short fat ones" (217). This brief comment initiates Leila into the knowledge of mortality, crushing, as a result, her youthful fantasy. Her hysteric cry "I want to stop" (218) ushers in the climactic moment of the narrative. Thus, with the aid of fantasy, the thematic development of initiation into knowledge and experience coincides with the structural development of narrative conflict.

In narrative structure, resolution usually follows the climactic clash. The endings in Mansfield's stories have led to the displeasure of some critics, who see them as abrupt and sometimes accidental, for they fail to offer plausible solutions to the tensions. Neither an extension of nor a termination to the narrative conflict, these types of endings, they believe, can only evince the author's lack of a sense of an over-all structural design. Criticism of this sort frequently results from a narrow interpretation of the meaning of "resolution." In stories where both narrative action and conflict are turned within the sphere of the human psyche, the resolution can be accordingly expressed in "moments of perception" (Bader 43). As the tension is built on the discrepancy between fantasy and reality, the resolution to the immediate conflict lies, therefore, in the characters' discovery and recognition of truth as opposed to illusion. When the narrative reaches this point of recognition, the battle of mind temporarily ceases, with the world of fantasy gradually conceding. That is, perhaps, what Bader means by "resolution... by implication" (43).

Resolution assumes two basic forms in Mansfield's stories. In the first, the subjective truth, or the little world of fantasy, is utterly shattered in its confrontation with the objective reality; and the protagonists, after experiencing the reversal of expectation, temporarily lose their bearing, but eventually recover with a new knowledge of life. Laura in "The Garden Party" certainly belongs there. In the second, the major characters are able to sustain the shock of the crushed dream by either transforming it into something positive, or creating a new world of fantasy. Two representative examples are "Her First Ball" and "The Doll's House."

As the resolution to the conflict is crucial in any thematically completed stories, the "central moment of realization" (Madden 5504A) becomes of primary importance in Mansfield's narrative structure. Mansfield herself is keenly aware of it as she makes the following comment:

> The crisis, then, is the chief of our "central points of significance" and the endeavours and the emotions are stages on our journey towards or away from it. For without it, the form of the novel, as we see it, is lost. Without it, how are we to appreciate the importance of one "spiritual event" rather than another? What is to prevent each being unrelated—complete in itself—if the gradual unfolding in growing, gaining light is not to be followed by one blazing moment? (*Novels and Novelists* 29–30)

This "blazing moment" is the one in which the character gains a sudden and new perception of life. The methods Mansfield adopts to weave the thematic motif of "escape-entrapment" (Madden 5504A) around this central epiphanic moment of realization reveal the process of how reality and fantasy react to each other. These methods fall roughly into Kathryn Hume's classification of the techniques of "literature of vision," that is, a literature which helps a "fictive world" to "comment on reality" (83). In Hume's analysis, these techniques are grouped into three types:

additive, subtractive, and contrastive. By "additive," she means that the world presented in vision or fantasy is "notably fuller, richer, and more varied and vivid than our everyday reality, or it reminds us that our own has much that we pass over unconsciously." The "subtractive" technique, on the other hand, constructs worlds which are "either very narrow definitions of reality" where "large portions of human experience" are left out, or where "the author has deliberately erased expected material, especially the logical connections between actions." The last of the three techniques creates contrastive worlds, "a special subset of the subtractive," which "refine[s] the complexity of reality down to two centers of interest; the tension between these two constitutes a comment on the nature of reality" (83). Hume's comment on literature of vision sheds light on the study of Mansfield's creative art, for, in her world of fiction, the various techniques by which fantasy is utilized to reinforce narrative structure produce the effects approximately as Hume predicts.

The additive or augmented world of which Hume speaks is a recurring form of fantasy in Mansfield's works, especially in the cluster of stories set in the author's mystic home country and centering on the Burnell and Sheridan families. In "At the Bay," the intended sequel to "Prelude," Mansfield uses this technique almost to perfection.

The loose connection of the kaleidoscopic events as witnessed both in "Prelude" and "At the Bay" has roused considerable amount of criticism on the over-all structural design. Marvin Magalaner, among other critics, has expressed his bewilderment in *The Fiction of Katherine Mansfield*:

> Mansfield's technique in the story [At the Bay] is even more maddeningly indifferent to the requirements of the contemporary explicator that a work of art be tightly constructed, each part of the thematic frame smoothly attaching to every other part, than even "Prelude" was. The relevance of each episode to the others is not always clear, and, in some instances probably does not reveal itself for the good reason that it is not there except in a nebulous, hazy fashion. (39)

Although not clear at first sight, the narrative structure in "At the Bay" has a tightness of its own which defies traditional approach. Most of the twelve episodes which constitute the main body of the narrative are structurally complete and self-contained units. When the individual episodic events consist themselves of action, conflict and resolution, stated or implied, they also combine to produce a larger thematic unity—the recurring motif in Mansfield's works: escape and entrapment. The episodes are linked to each other not by apparent logical connection, but by a unifying time and spatial framework where fantasy and reality reign in turn. The twelve events are arranged in a concentric pattern with the Crescent Bay as the axis and a twenty-four-hour duration the circumference. Magalaner's bewilderment is not fully justifiable, because the taxing task of making up the omitted logical linking is now left by the more demanding modern author to her more sophisticated modern reader.

"At the Bay" is a controversial story. Cherry Hankin, for example, insists on its superiority to "Prelude" because

> what Katherine Mansfield needed to plumb now was not so much the mysterious depths of human relationships: it was the mysterious ebb and flow of life itself. The death which she faced alone had to be seen in the wider, universal perspective of the death—and renewal—of all natural forms. Thus individual suffering, individual regret, give way in this story [At the Bay] to a greater but shared pain at the knowledge of life's shortness. (*Confessional Stories* 223)

The wider and more profound subject matter needs a more sophisticated narrative structure. As the complex web of human relationships has faded into a less prominent position, thematic conflict and the resultant narrative climax are now centered on "inertia" and "exploration" (Hankin *Confessional Stories* 231), which divide and regroup the major characters. The divergence in their fundamental attitude towards life originates, ironically, from their common realization of life's transience. Distinctively marked with either lassitude or vitality, they generally employ fantasy as an aid to augment their limited possibilities in reality.

The conflict between inertia and exploration is revealed very early in the story through a contrastive philosophy of life held by characters such as Linda, Beryl, Stanley and Jonathan. As in "Prelude," Linda still bears the grudge against the role of wife and mother, although her bitterness is now diluted with a slight sense of humor:

> There were glimpses, moments, breathing spaces of calm, but all the rest of the time it was like living in a house that couldn't be cured of the habit of catching on fire, on a ship that got wrecked every day. And it was always Stanley who was in the thick of the danger. Her whole time was spent in rescuing him, and restoring him, and calming him down, and listening to his story. And what was left of her time was spent in the dread of having children. (*The Garden Party and Other Stories* 33)

Linda's grudge against the senselessness of the daily existence is made even more acute by her awareness of life's fragility. A sense of fundamental helplessness creeps in as she watches the flowers blossoming in her garden while "dreaming the morning away" (30):

> If only one had time to look at these flowers long enough, time to get over the sense of novelty and strangeness, time to know them! But as soon as one paused to part the petals, to discover the under-side of the leaf, along came Life and one was swept away. And, lying in her cane chair, Linda felt so light; she felt like a leaf. Along came Life like a wind and she was seized and shaken; she had to go. Oh, dear, would it always be so? Was there no escape? (32)

Here, Linda's wish to escape the unwilling role of wife and mother gives way to a universal human desire to flee from the grip of death. The conflict between her and Stanley, continued from "Prelude," has now transcended the narrow confines of sexuality and extended to their attitude towards life itself. Her lassitude in the story encompasses a wide range of meanings, among which is the gesture for preserving life. To her, engagement in any substantial physical actions is to commit the crime of energy consumption. The household chore, the expected sexual obligations, and worst of all, the child-birth trauma, are the very things that shorten the already limited life span.

Antithetical to Linda's lassitude is Stanley's vivacity. Equally aware of life's shortness, he fights the approaching shadow of death by making positive use of every minute, and his whole existence is defined by physical actions—working, sporting, eating, and an excessive enjoyment of sex. Stanley's role here has exceeded that of a mere sexual predator as in "Prelude," for his presence signifies now an immediate threat to Linda's very sense of existence.

Linda's physical languor seems simultaneously to contrast and accelerate her mental activities, for she is virtually the greatest dreamer in the story. Her fantasy includes a whole range of experiences, expanding her limited reality of existence. By recapturing her childhood dream of exploration, for example, she is able to compensate for her life deprived of any substantial activities:

> ... Now she sat on the veranda of their Tasmanian home, leaning against her father's knee. And he promised, "As soon as you and I are old enough, Linny, we'll cut off somewhere, we'll escape. Two boys together. I have a fancy I'd like to sail up a river in China." Linda saw that river, very wide, covered with little rafts and boats. She saw the yellow hats of the boatmen and she heard their high, thin voices as they called... (32)

Thus, the conflict between inertia and exploration is revealed not only through Linda's love-hate relationship with Stanley, but also through the disparity between her dream of adventure and the reality of a static married life. The conflict with Stanley does not aggravate into a complete rupture not because Linda "rediscovers her love for him" and "accepts... his foibles," as Hankin tries to convince us (*Confessional Stories* 233), but because of her recognition of the insignificance of human efforts in face of the invincibility and inevitability of the law of life. Also contributive to her gesture of acceptance is fantasy's complementary and supplementary function which offers her a fuller interpretation of the meaning of her confined reality. The narrative conflict is resolved, therefore, through Linda's acknowledgment of frustration, for disillusionment "offers a powerful challenge to our mind-sets and outlooks" and "reminds us of our freedom" (Hume 126).

For Linda, the epiphanic moment of realization is also found in her relationship with her baby son. While in actual life, she cannot share Stanley's pride in their son and heir, in fantasy the presence of the boy enriches her understanding of the essence of life. In episode VI during her morning reveries, she imagines a heart-to-heart talk with the baby, whose intuitive faith in life stirs up a stab of love in her:

> Linda was so astonished at the confidence of this little creature.... Ah, no, be sincere. That was not what she felt; it was something far different, it was something so new, so... The tear danced in her eyes; she breathed in a small whisper to the boy, "Hallo, my funny!" (35)

Here again fantasy enters to achieve the resolution to the thematic conflict. Linda's acceptance of, and eventually, the love for, the boy, comes with her recognition of the inevitability of life's metabolism. Yet this knowledge is instilled to her not through her daily contact with reality, but through the whimsical moment of fantasy. When viewed in fantasy, the baby, no longer a malicious force threatening to shorten her life, becomes a continuation and renewal of her own existence.

In "At the Bay," while the major thematic conflict discloses itself mainly through Linda's ambivalent attitude towards Stanley and her children, other characters, such as Beryl Fairfield and Jonathan Trout, are also drawn into the vortex, torn between a desire for adventure and the expected social roles which prevent them from so doing. In the complex Burnell family organization, Beryl stands between her sister Linda and brother-in-law Stanley, sharing the former's habit of day-dreaming and the latter's love for physical activities. The conflict of exploration and inertia is reflected in her eager indulgence in fantasy for emotional adventure and her fear of her own dreams when they threaten to substitute reality. Here as in "Prelude," Beryl is allowed "only one avenue to happiness"—respectable marriage (Fullbrook 112), for her entire social identity is defined by the acquisition of a husband. Like

Linda, she wraps herself up in fantasy, a supplement to her emotionally arid life and the only means she can dream of a social recognition through her own efforts. In her imaginative conversation with the bush, after a day's adventure at the beach with Mrs. Kember, she betrays her longing for a speedy delivery from the crisis of life by a fantasized lover:

> "Take me away from all these other people, my love. Let us go far away. Let us live our life, all new, all ours, from the very beginning. Let us make our fire. Let us sit down to eat together. Let us have long talks at night."
>
> And the thought was almost, "Save me, my love. Save me!" (63)

Her relationship with the Kembers is an extended part of her dream world. Richard F. Peterson in "The Circle of Truth" mistakenly suggests that the major "disruption or flaw" of the story "comes from outside the family circle. " "Mansfield's introduction of the Kembers into the Burnells' pattern of existence," he holds, "creates the dark and threatening atmosphere... and separates its vision of life from that in 'Prelude'" (389). Beryl's adventure with the Kembers, instead of loosening the narrative structure centering on the Burnell family, adds another dimension to their established order of life. It also reinforces the effect of thematic conflict because of its revelation of Beryl's love and fear for exploration all at the same time. This relationship constitutes a part of Beryl's fantasized attempt to adventure into the strange realm of sexuality. But she quickly withdraws when fantasy threatens to substitute rather than augment reality. In the last scene of the story, her shrinking from physical contacts with Harry Kember is a fleeing from "simultaneously her own desire and its fulfillment, and a victimization that would distortedly enact the marriage she needs for personal validation" (Fullbrook 113).

While Linda's inertia is formed as a part of her married life, Beryl's desire for action originates from a need for change, namely, a marriage. Thus, as the thematic conflict develops on the divergence in their fundamental view towards life, Linda's bondage becomes Beryl's means of liberation. The resolution to the tension and crisis in Beryl's situation also depends upon her recognition of frustration and defeat. In her hasty escape from the embrace of the odious Harry Kember, she has demonstrated her acknowledgment of dream's inadequacy in substituting reality. The temporary restoration of peace following this implied resolution marks the conclusion of the narrative, again with a reference to the sea, but now in its nightly serenity:

> A cloud, small, serene, floated across the moon. In that moment of darkness the sea sounded deep, troubled. Then the cloud sailed away, and the sound of the sea was a vague murmur, as though it waked out of a dark dream. All was still. (67)

If in "At the Bay," fantasy assists to achieve the structural completeness by supplementing reality, its function in "Miss Brill" is primarily to build up tension by intensifying the heroine's restricted vision of life and then proving it as totally mistaken. It is obvious that the general structural design of the two stories differs drastically. While the former is constructed in episodic pieces "according to the demands of symbolic patterning" (Hanson and Gurr 76), the latter adheres more closely to the rule of unity of action, time, and space. The structural disparity is brought about not only by different arrangement of narrative units, or episodic events, but also by the different ways in which fantasy enters and, subsequently, affects the theme.

The world Miss Brill fabricates in fantasy is a "subtractive" one, using Hume's standard. Instead of enriching and expanding her view, her dreams tend to define life in very narrow terms which "leave out large portions of human experience" (Hume 83). A poor and aging maid in exile, she feeds herself on a neurotic and fantastic imagination that her presence matters in the life of other people. The thematic conflict between stasis and vitality, and illusion and reality, as we discover in "At the Bay," is here extended to that of "age and youth," and "solitude and community" (Hanson and Gurr 77). As the story is narrated strictly from the heroine's consciousness, this conflict is not made explicit to the reader until, towards the end of the story, Miss Brill discovers for herself the gulf between the dreamy expectation and the shattering reality.

Miss Brill's illusory notion of life and her false sense of community combine to establish a part of the major narrative conflict. In her confined point of view, existence is defined exclusively by the appearance of youth, vitality, and a communal acceptance. One symptom of her mind restriction is her obsessive fondness of the shabby fur piece, a sign of life to her:

> Dear little thing! It was nice to feel it again. She had taken it out of its box that afternoon, shaken out the moth-powder, given it a good brush, and rubbed the life back into the dim little eyes. "What has been happening to me?" said the sad little eyes. Oh, how sweet it was to see them snap at her again from the elder-down! …. Little rogue! Yes, she really felt like that about it. Little rogue biting its tail just by her left ear. She could have taken it off and laid it on her lap and stroked it. She felt a tingling in her hands and arms, but that came from walking, she supposed. (*The Garden Party and Other Stories* 199–200)

This fantasized personification of the fur piece reveals the title heroine's excessive consciousness of and uncertainty about life. Her explicit reluctance to repair the nose of the fur until it is "absolutely necessary" (200) further externalizes her unwillingness to acknowledge her faded youth. She needs an external object and a communal support to confirm her own existence, which also accounts for her frequent visits to the park.

Fantasy continues to dominate the scene as Miss Brill arrives in Jardins Publiques to enjoy the concert as well as the eavesdropping. She asserts her own importance by fantasizing the whole setting as a huge stage and herself an actress whose presence is felt:

> Oh, how fascinating it was! How she enjoyed it! How she loved sitting there, watching it all! It was like a play. It was exactly like a play…. They were all on the stage. They weren't only the audience, not only looking on; they were acting. Even she had a part and came every Sunday. No doubt somebody would have noticed if she hadn't been there; she was part of the performance after all. (204)

Her false notion of vitality and fellowship foreshadows and intensifies the climactic clash which is delayed until the end of the narrative. The indifference and incompatibility of the people towards each other at the park do not register with her. In her fantastic imagination, she thinks that she shares a comradeship with all of them as they hustle and bustle across the stage of life. This illusion is ultimately peeled off when the real hero and heroine enter the "theater" and explicitly express their disgust towards her:

> "No, not now," said the girl. "Not here, I can't."
> "But why? Because of that stupid old thing at the end there?" asked the boy. "Why does she come here at all—who wants her? Why doesn't she keep her silly old mug at home?" (206)

The effect of this "catastrophic descent from illusory pleasure" (Daly 90) is dramatically heightened, first because it is revealed from Miss Brill's own viewpoint, and, secondly, because it smashes the world which contains the whole meaning of her existence. When she overhears the conversation, she finally realizes the insignificance of her own existence, or indeed, any individual existence, to the human society as a whole. This epiphanic moment of truth ushers in the resolution to the major thematic conflict, for the tension is temporarily eased as the heroine, after experiencing the crushing of dream, ironically rediscovers her courage to face the cruelty of isolation. No longer feigning young and contesting for public attention, she hastily returns home, a changed woman:

> She sat there for a long time. The box that the fur came out of was on the bed. She unclasped the necklet quickly; quickly, without looking, laid it inside. But when she put the lid on, she thought she heard something crying. (207)

Metaphorically, what she has shut in her dingy lonely room is not the box containing the fur piece, but the rosy dream of life. With the box closed, she bids her farewell to the fantasy world. Now a woman prepared to face the unpleasant solitary reality, she suddenly finds in her a growing sense of fortitude and dignity.

This climactic moment and the attendant resolution are, nevertheless, marred by a tinge of contrivance. Here as in "Bliss," while the fantasized vision of life is capable of stirring up the reader's pathos, it is the reality that seems "arranged," leaving "a lasting impression, not of life, but of the author's cleverness" (Peterson 385).

Whereas fantasy functions in "Miss Brill" as a "subtractive," in the architecture of "The Garden Party," a masterpiece in Mansfield's canon, it forms one of the two contrastive poles of the narrative. The story's major conflict revolves around these two poles of interest—the upper-class Sheridan household and its glamorous social occasion counter-posing the poverty-stricken neighborhood and the tragic death of a poor carter. Critics have sometimes overemphasized the significance of the death, treating it as the center of the thematic structure. Such reading has obviously distorted Mansfield's declared aim to depict "the diversity of life and how we try to fit in everything, **Death included**" [emphasis mine] (*Letters* 454). Although the poor carter's death definitely marks a milestone in the young heroine's metaphoric journey from innocence to knowledge, the story is primarily concerned with "the grace of living and the disgrace of existence" (Hormasji 115).

Unlike many of Mansfield's stories where the narrative action mainly consists of flashing moments of revelation, the thematic conflict in "The Garden Party" is developed on a series of mental as well as physical activities focusing on the Sheridans' social gathering. The demarcation between the Sheridans, the dream world of gaiety and splendors, and the Scotts, the representative of the sordid aspects of reality, is both physical and metaphorical. The antithetical poles leading to the story's climactic clash are essentially constructed on the time, spatial, and atmospheric difference which separates these two worlds.

The narrative action starts with a series of preparations for the Sheridans' garden party. The Sheridans' habitual indulgence in fantasy immediately professes itself through the way they arrange the party. The tone in which Mansfield depicts the garden reveals her mocking attitude towards the Sheridans' life style. Obviously, the garden is not a perfect paradise "beyond the bounds of time and space" with a "natural abundance," as Anders Iversen suggests in "A Reading of Katherine Mansfield's 'The Garden Party'" (8–9). The sense of dreamy artificiality saturates their household where nature can be "ordered" and methodized according to their schedule (*The Garden Party and Other Stories* 68). The careful arrangement of the lawn, the flowers and the marquee are only a part of their efforts to remold their natural environment, with a sole aim of impressing.

This sense of artificiality, as a part of the Sheridans' fantasy play, also includes Laura's attempt to mimic her mother's voice while talking to the workmen; Jose's imitation of her parents' manners in giving orders to the servants, and finally, her sentimental rendering of the song: "This Life is **Wee**—ary, / Hope comes to Die. / A Dream—a **Wa**—kening" (77).

The unnaturalness of the setting undermines the ostensible signs of nature and vitality, making everything that comes within its compass illusory and fantastic. The long passages devoted to the Sheridans' dreamy anticipation of the party are aimed, structurally speaking, to prepare the reader for the other pole of life, the real crisis beneath the surface of happiness. Laura, being the artistic one in the family, has a greater capacity for dreaming. Using her power of imagination, she transforms the "tiny spots of sun" on the inkpot lid into "a warm little silver star" (74). With the same power, she romanticizes the workmen who come to set up the marquee into "fairy princes" in distress (71–72).

Thus, in her sentimentalization, the workmen, "from being less than ordinary human beings," have now "become more than human" (Iversen 11). Despite her self-deceptive vision that "these absurd class distinctions" matter "not an atom" to her (72), she cannot refrain from speaking condescendingly to them, trying to "look severe and even a little short-sighted" (69) at them and wondering "whether it was quite respectful of a workman to talk to her of bangs slap in the eye" (70). Her instant attraction to the working class is triggered more by the sense of novelty, a natural consequence of her sheltered butterfly life. Yet her sentimentalization is cut short as the story takes a drastic turn.

The first, albeit false, narrative climax takes place when the news of the accident reaches Laura in the kitchen. From the culmination of bliss she is thrown into the depth of confusion. This shattering moment, however, is evanescent, for she is then shocked by the hearsay of death only. The sorrow and indignation roused by the knowledge of death and the heartlessness of her family are soon blurred away at the prospect of the party:

> Just for a moment she had another glimpse of that poor woman and those little children, and the body being carried into the house. But it all seemed blurred, unreal, like a picture in the newspaper. I'll remember it again after the party's over, she decided. And somehow that seemed quite the best plan. (84)

As Laura decides to yield to fantasy, the unpleasant fact of poverty and death fades into a "blurred" and "unreal" background whereas the contrived garden party remains the only tangible reality. Although the indulgence in dreams is a shared feature of all the Sheridan females, they unite to oppose it if it threatens to go to excess. When, for example, Laura impulsively tries to stop the party at the news of the accident, she is condemned by her mother and sisters as "absurd" and "extravagant" (84). To them, there is only one thin partition between imagination and absurdity, as is evident by "the easiness with which a character can be thrust from full membership of a community to absolute exile in an instant" (Fullbrook 123).

The first climactic clash between the fantasized vision of happiness and the approaching shadow of death is followed soon by the second as Laura is literally and figuratively forced out to face actual death. It is not until almost four fifths of the story is over that the other of the two antithetical poles of the narrative structure—the dark underworld of the working neighbors—is introduced to the reader.

Laura's trip to the Scotts' becomes more psychological than physical as the contrastive role of the two worlds grows overt. The young heroine's light-hearted happiness, already tinged by a vague shadow of the hearsay death, gradually yields to an apprehension and even a fear as she leaves her garden of artificial abundance for the gloomy lane where the workers reside:

> Now the broad road was crossed. The lane began, smoky and dark. Women in shawls and men's tweed caps hurried by. Men hung over the palings; the children played in the doorways. A low hum came from the mean little cottages. In some of them there was a flicker of light, and a shadow, crab-like, moved across the window. Laura bent her head and hurried on. She wished now she had put on a coat. How her frock shone! And the big hat with velvet streamer—if only it was another hat! Were the people looking at her? They must be. It was a mistake to have come…. (89)

The contrast is not only spatial but also temporal. It is early morning when Laura and her sisters are preparing, with eager anticipation, for the garden party. But when Laura starts for the Scotts, "the perfect afternoon" has been "slowly ripened, slowly faded, and its petals closed" (86). The lane is a world of dusk which thrusts into Laura's consciousness the knowledge of hardship, sorrow and death. Death's "foreignness" is responsible, as Adam J. Sorkin perceptively points out, for her over-reaction:

> It is wealth's particular psychological effect to blur poverty and death and likewise to distance and ritualize mortality until it seems unusual news from elsewhere, certainly (as in the case) from outside the false paradise of the garden. (446)

The real climactic moment is reached at the very end of the narrative in Laura's face-to-face encounter with death. Yet she has not "waken from her dream-life, the existence of garden parties and Sheridan exclusivity" through the "contact with death," as Magalaner suggests (*The Fiction of Katherine Mansfield* 117). Shocked and confused as she is, she hastily accepts death as a part, not of reality, but of dream. The dead carter is consequently romanticized into another prince figure in her fantasy tales:

> There lay a young man, fast asleep—sleeping so soundly, so deeply, that he was far, far away from them both. Oh, so remote, so peaceful. He was dreaming. Never wake him up again. His head was sunk in the pillow, his eyes were closed; they were blind under the closed eyelids. He was given up to his dream. What did garden-parties and baskets and lace frocks matter to him? …. He was wonderful, beautiful…. Happy... happy…. All is well, said that sleeping face. (91–92)

Through fantasizing, Laura is able to ease the shock of death, but her dream vision has now acquired a more extensive dimension. She returns to the Sheridan garden, a changed and wiser girl, for she has partially escaped the ideological narrowness of this false paradise with a new knowledge of life including the awareness of mortality. This new knowledge, the exact content of which she fails to explain, marks her first entrance into womanhood and a temporary resolution to the tension that constitutes the pain of growing up. The worlds of the Sheridans and the Scotts are relatively reconciled through Laura's appreciation of beauty which transcends the gulf between the two worlds. Just as this new knowledge of life is more implicit than explicit, so is the resolution to the narrative conflict more implied than stated.

Thus, from "At the Bay," "Miss Brill," "The Garden Party" and a number of other stories, we see a relatively consistent narrative pattern which draws upon fantasy for structural reinforcement. The accusation that Mansfield's works are formless is not completely justified, for the essential component elements of narrative structure, that is, action, conflict and resolution, are still there, despite the different manner of presentation. Although fantasy brings in innovative interpretation of the concept of time and space and shifts plot, conflict, and resolution into the realm of individual psyche, the characters and events are still dynamic because the nature of narrative action and conflict remains unchanged.

The major structural functions of fantasy in Mansfield's works, as we discover in the stories examined previously, are additive, subtractive or contrastive. In the additive, the author introduces fantasy into the plot to augment her protagonists' limited experience. The narrative conflict revolves around their vacillation between the love for day-dreaming and the fear for dream's substitution of reality. The resolution to the conflict lies either in their temporary feeling of content in the supplementary world which fantasy creates or their open confession of frustration and defeat, as in the case of Linda and Beryl in "At the Bay."

In its subtractive function, fantasy enters the scene by narrowing the heroines' outlook into a very exclusive interpretation of life. The narrative conflict is intensified into a climactic clash as reality suddenly intrudes into, and ultimately crushes, this world of exclusivity. The climactic moment is usually followed by an implied resolution as the victim, no longer able to cling to fantasy as a mainstay of existence, is virtually forced to face bare reality, just like the title heroines in "Miss Brill" and "The Little Governess."

Fantasy also reinforces the narrative structure by constructing, through its confrontation with reality, two antithetical poles composed of contrastive values. The confusion of the characters, as they are caught between the two worlds, constitutes the major part of the plot and the narrative conflict. The epiphanic moment of realization is the one in which the characters discover, as in "The Garden Party" and "Marriage A La Mode," not an immediate solution to their confusion, but a new philosophy of life which transcends their established concept of truth.

CHAPTER V

CONCLUSION

In discussing the art of the short story, Edgar Allan Poe isolates "the unity of effect" as "a point of the greatest importance." Without a certain continuity of effort, he maintains, "the soul is never deeply moved" (2). Katherine Mansfield herself is also aware of this "importance" as she confesses to Richard Murry, her artist brother-in-law, that she possesses "a passion for technique, … for making the things into a whole" (*Letters* 364). This passion Eileen Baldeshwiler interprets, in the terminology of modern literary criticism, as a dislike for "a plethora of details not responsible to a… deeper significance," which "results only in a dissipation of total impression" (426). The "continuity of effort" to which Poe refers assumes the form of the recurrent fantasy scenes in Mansfield's fiction. Despite her occasional changes in subject matter and shifts in perspectives, fantasy has remained a consistent feature and a part of her theme, characterization, symbolism, as well as narrative structure. From her earliest juvenilia, such as "His Ideal" and "My Potplant," to her swan songs including "Ma Parker" and "The Doll's House," Mansfield has persistently endeavored to employ fantasy as a means both of exploring and of commenting on the nature of reality.

However, this "continuity of effort" alone does not necessarily produce "the unity of effect" or the artistic "whole," of which both Poe and Mansfield speak. In her earlier works, for example, Mansfield's intended goal to examine reality through its reflection in fantasy is frequently interrupted and even distorted because of her heroines' over-indulgence in day-dreaming. The "total impression," or general effect, of the narrative is dissipated, as the fictive world, instead of commenting upon reality, almost blots out the empirical world completely. Thus the means originally employed to achieve the end unwittingly defeats the end. Such examples can be found in "Something Childish but Very Natural" and "The Little Governess," where the protagonists' fantasy world seldom, if ever, relates to their empirical environment.

In Mansfield's more mature works, fantasy contributes to making the nature of reality manifest. According to Robert Scholes and Robert Kellogg:

> …meaning, in a work of narrative art, is a function of the relationship between two worlds: the fictional world created by the author and the "real" world, the apprehendable universe. When we say we "understand" a narrative we mean that we have found a satisfactory relationship or set of relationships between these two worlds. (82)

Here "fictional" and "satisfactory" can be more appropriately substituted with "fantasy" and "revelatory." In most of Mansfield's later stories, the "continuity of effort" to reveal the nature of reality through fantasy eventually results in "the unity of effect" because a set of relationships between the two are established and examined. Sometimes, the author sets fantasy as an antithesis to reality by exposing the impossibility of its realization in mimetic environment, an example of which is Laura's fancy of becoming one of the working class in "The Garden Party." At other times, fantasy functions as a supplement to the characters' incomplete experience, exploring what they may have achieved under altered circumstances, such as Linda's and Beryl's dreams about change in the New Zealand stories. In some of her most successful works, Mansfield creates a world which is virtually the synthesis of the fictive and the mimetic. The mimetic setting reveals the truth of facts whereas fantasy discloses the truth of feelings. Through the interaction between the two, the reader is given access to the knowledge of both the objective and the subjective reality.

Fantasy, as a special fictional technique, also adds realistic depth to Mansfield's narratives. Two basic features in her use of fantasy have sufficiently established it as an inseparable aspect of "serious literature"—the sincerity in the characters' pursuit of beauty and truth, and the indignation against the brutality of human existence.

As early as 1918, Mansfield has attributed her impulse to write to "two kick-offs." One is "real joy" or "that state of being in some perfectly blissful way **at peace**;" the other is "an **extremely** deep sense of helplessness, of everything doomed to disaster" or "**a cry against corruption**" (*Letters to Murry* 149). These two "kick-offs" explain the soul's travail of her characters as well as the nature of their fantasy.

Human relationship as presented in her stories is a complicated one, for most of her protagonists are brutalized by "the one most loved, most trusted" (Zinman 458). The exploitation by insensitive sexual partners or tyrannical parents, experienced by Linda in "Prelude" and "At the Bay," Miss Moss in "Pictures" and Constantia and Josephine in "The Daughters of the Late Colonel," constitutes the major agony of her female characters.

The pain of life, however, is not inflicted upon women alone. Some of her male characters are also depicted as struggling in the miserable dilemma of life or victimized by the female world which centers on vanity and snobbery, such as the pitiful hero in "The Man Without A Temperament" and the manipulated husband in "Marriage A La Mode." The old are victims, too. They subsist on their memories of their faded youth, striving to come to grips with the fact of age and death, like the heroine in "Miss Brill" and the protagonists in "Ma Parker" and "The Fly." The young and innocent, on the other hand, have to pay dearly for their impulse to adventure into the realm of knowledge and experience, like Leila in "Her First Ball" and the heroine in "The Little Governess." As most of these characters are weak, trapped, and helpless, the only way for them to articulate their desire and indignation is through fantasy.

Fantasy in Mansfield's works reveals two aspects of human nature: the natural desire for something better and the natural repulsion against the ugliness or "the cry against corruption." These two are often knitted closely together. When the desire for beauty and truth, sometimes expressed in an illusory feeling of bliss, ends in inevitable disappointment and even disillusionment, the characters' voice deepens into rage and indignation. Bertha's confused wondering in "Bliss" can be seen as an extension of Laura's eager quest for the meaning of life in "The Garden Party." Beryl's restless longing for personal validation and Linda's dream of escaping the trap of marriage may simply result in Miss Brill's fear of age and isolation and Ma Parker's outcry against the brutality of human condition. Their dreams betray both their sincerity in searching for life's better alternatives and their agony at the failures. These features of fantasy reveal the deep truth of humanity and help to establish Mansfield as one of the serious writers of the twentieth century.

WORKS CITED AND CONSULTED

Primary Sources

Mansfield, Katherine. *Bliss and Other Stories*. London: Constable, 1920.

—. *The Critical Writings of Katherine Mansfield*. Ed. Clare Hanson. Houndmills: Macmillan, 1987.

—. *The Doves' Nest and Other Stories*. London: Constable, 1923.

—. *The Garden Party and Other Stories*. Toronto: Macmillan, 1922.

—. *Journals of Katherine Mansfield*. Ed. John Middleton Murry. Definitive ed. London: Constable, 1954.

—. *The Letters of Katherine Mansfield*. Ed. John Middleton Murry. New York: Howard Fertig, 1929.

—. *Letters of Katherine Mansfield to John Middleton Murry (1913–1922)*. Ed. John Middleton Murry. London: Constable, 1951.

—. *Novels and Novelists*. Ed. John Middleton Murry. London: Constable, 1930.

—. *The Scrapbook of Katherine Mansfield*. Ed. John Middleton Murry. New York: Alfred A. Knopf, 1940.

—. *Something Childish and Other Stories*. London: Constable, 1924.

Secondary Sources

Abrams, M. H. *A Glossary of Literary Terms*. 3rd ed. New York: Holt, Rinehart and Winston, 1971.

Alpers, Antony. *The Life of Katherine Mansfield*. London: Jonathan Cape, 1980.

Anderson, Walter E. "The Hidden Love Triangle in Mansfield's 'Bliss'." *Twentieth Century Literature* 28 (1982 winter): 397–404.

Bader, Arnold. "The Structure of the Modern Short Story." *Discussions of the Short Story*. Ed. Hollis Summers. Boston: D. C. Health & Company, 1963: 40–45.

Baldeshwiler, Eileen. "Katherine Mansfield's Theory of Fiction." *Studies in Short Fiction* 7 (1970): 421–32.

Bardas, Mary L. "The State of Scholarship on Katherine Mansfield, 1950–1970." *World Literature Written in English* 11.1 (1972): 77–93.

Bates, H. E. *The Modern Short Story: Critical Survey*. London: Thomas Nelson & Sons, 1941.

Beachcroft, T. O. "Katherine Mansfield—Then and Now." *Modern Fiction Studies* 24 (1978): 343–52.

Berkman, Sylvia. *Katherine Mansfield: A Critical Study*. New Haven: Yale University Press, 1951.

Bowen, Elizabeth. "Katherine Mansfield." *Discussions of the Short Story*. Ed. Hollis Summers. Boston: D. C. Health & company, 1963: 89–93.

Bowling, David Hurst. "Katherine Mansfield: Her Theory and Practice of Fiction." *Dissertation Abstracts International* 39 (1978): 2254A.

Daly, Saralyn R. *Katherine Mansfield*. New York: Twayne Publishers, 1965.

Delany, Paul. "Short and Simple Annals of the Poor: Katherine Mansfield's 'The Doll's House'." *Mosaic* 10. i: 7–17.

Eisinger, Chester. "Mansfield's 'Bliss'." *Explicator* 7 (1949): item 48.

Forster, E. M. *Aspects of the Novel*. 1927. Harmondsworth: Penguin Books, 1954.

Fullbrook, Kate. *Katherine Mansfield*. Bloomington and Indianapolis: Indiana University Press, 1986.

Gold, Herbert. A Talk to the "International Symposium on the Short Story." *Kenyon Review* 30 (1968): 450–54.

Gordimer, Nadine. A Talk to the "International Symposium on the Short Story." *Kenyon Review* 30 (1968): 457–63.

Gurr, Andrew. *Writers in Exile: The Identity of Home in Modern Literature*. Sussex: Harvester Press, 1981.

Hankin, Cherry. "Fantasy and the Sense of an Ending in the Work of Katherine Mansfield." *Modern Fiction Studies* 24 (1978): 465–74.

— . *Katherine Mansfield and Her Confessional Stories*. London: Macmillan, 1983.

Hanson, Clare. "Introduction." *The Critical Writings of Katherine Mansfield.* Houndmills: Macmillan, 1987.

—, and Andrew Gurr. *Katherine Mansfield.* London: Macmillan, 1981.

Hormasji, Nariman. *Katherine Mansfield: An Appraisal.* London: Collins, 1967.

Hume, Kathryn. *Fantasy and Mimesis: Responses to Reality in Western Literature.* New York & London: Methuen, 1984.

Iversen, Anders. "A Reading of Katherine Mansfield's 'The Garden Party'." *Orbis Litterarum* 23 (1968): 5–34.

King, Russell S. "Katherine Mansfield as an Expatriate Writer." *Journal of Commonwealth Literature* 8.1 (1973): 97–109.

Madden, Fred Stanley. "The Development of a Consistent Structural Pattern in Katherine Mansfield's Short Stories." *Dissertation Abstracts International* 39 (1979): 5504A–05A.

Magalaner, Marvin. *The Fiction of Katherine Mansfield.* Carbondale and Edwardsville: Southern Illinois University Press, 1971.

—. "Traces of Her 'Self' in Katherine Mansfield's 'Bliss'." *Modern Fiction Studies* 24 (1978): 413–22.

Mantz, Ruth Elvish, and John Middleton Murry. *The Life of Katherine Mansfield.* London: Constable, 1933.

Maxwell-Mahon, W. D. "The Art of Katherine Mansfield." *Unisa English Studies* 17. i: 45–52.

Meyers, Jeffrey. *Katherine Mansfield: A Biography*. London: Hamish Hamilton, 1978.

—. "Katherine Mansfield: A Selected Checklist." *Modern Fiction Studies* 24 (1978): 475–77.

Moore, Leslie. *Katherine Mansfield: the Memories of LM*. New York: Taplinger, 1971.

Murry, John Middleton. *Between Two Worlds: an Autobiography*. London: Jonathan Cape, 1935.

—. *Katherine Mansfield and Other Literary Studies*. London: Constable, 1959.

Neaman, Judith S. "Allusion, Image and Associative Pattern: The Answers in Mansfield's 'Bliss'." *Twentieth Century Literature* 32 (1986 Summer): 242–54.

Perry, F. M. *The Art of Story-writing*. London: G. Bell & Sons, 1926.

Peterson, Richard F. "The Circle of Truth: The Stories of Katherine Mansfield and Mary Lavin." *Modern Fiction Studies* 24 (1978): 383–412.

Poe, Edgar Allan. "Review of Twice-Told Tales." *Discussions of the Short Story*. Ed. Hollis Summers. Boston: D. C. Health & Company, 1963: 1–4.

Scholes, Robert, and Robert Kellogg. *The Nature of Narrative*. New York: Oxford University Press, 1966.

Showalter, Elaine. *A Literature of Their Own: British Women Novelists from Bronte to Lessing*. Princeton: Princeton University Press, 1977.

Sorkin, Adam J. "Katherine Mansfield's 'The Garden Party': Style and Social Occasion." *Modern Fiction Studies* 24 (1978): 439–55.

Stone, Jean E. "New Light on Katherine Mansfield." *Quadrant* 133: 43–47.

Summers, Hollis, ed. *Discussions of the Short Story*. Boston: D. C. Health & Company, 1963.

Surmelian, Leon. *Techniques of Fiction Writing: Measure and Madness*. Garden City: Doubleday & Company, 1969.

Walkerdine, Valerie. "The Thorn Birds: Fiction, Fantasy, Femininity." *Formations of Fantasy*. Ed. Victor Burgin, et al. London: Methuen, 1986.

Ward, Alfred C. *Aspects of the Modern Short Story: English and American*. London: University of London Press, 1924.

Willa, Cather. *Not Under Forty*. New York: Alfred A. Knopf, 1967.

Woolf, Virginia. *The Diary of Virginia Woolf*. Ed. Anne Olivier Bell. 2 vols. London: Hogarth, 1977.

Zapf, Hubert. "Time and Space in Katherine Mansfield's 'The Garden Party'." *Orbis Litterarum* 40.1 (1985): 44–54.

Zinman, Toby Silverman. "The Snail Under the Leaf: Katherine Mansfield's Imagery." *Modern Fiction Studies* 24 (1978): 457–64.

中文部分

摘　要

　　幻想元素的反复运用是凯瑟琳·曼斯菲尔德（Katherine Mansfield）小说艺术中有待进一步探研的领域之一。赫伯特·戈尔德（Herbert Gold）将幻想定义为"对生活可能性的梦想，它使人带有人性"（450），但纳丁·戈迪默（Nadine Gordimer）则认为它是"角度的变化"和"观察终极现实的更广阔的视角"（459—460）。凯瑟琳·休姆（Kathryn Hume）更概括性地认为，幻想是"**任何对公认的现实的背离**……其表现形式多种多样，从怪物到隐喻不等"（21）。曼斯菲尔德本人将幻想归因于艺术家想"在这个世界里创造自己的世界"的愿望（*Journal* 273）。被伦敦文坛排斥的局外人感受、在婚姻和同性恋女友之间的长期踌蹰不决，以及第一次世界大战的影响，是导致她转向内心世界的三大缘由。

　　幻想在曼斯菲尔德的小说中首先起到强化人物塑造的作用。当她对一个统一自我的存在持有将信将疑的双重态度时，她笔下那些既沉湎于角色扮演又渴望实现"真实"自我的人物，便陷入了两种欲望相互撕扯的困境之中。在他们的主观愿景不断地侵入客观现实时，幻想就成为人物塑造的一个部分。曼斯菲尔德通过对角色丰富经历的描写，为读者提供了探究人物内心世界的多重视角。

　　曼斯菲尔德多次说过，她偏爱通过各种带有暗示意味的姿势来显示灵魂的启示。她的幻想世界是由一系列带有丰富联想意义的意象所组成的。她早期的作品主要聚焦于某个"梦幻人物"，而她后期的作品则通过自然世界来完成比喻性的表述。她在幻想王国里所呈现的各种意象和象征，都展示了生活中备受争议的一个侧面：人类对真理和爱情不可遏制的渴求，以及无法实现渴求时所产生的绝望，这二者如影相随。

她小说的叙事框架既有背离传统的一面，也有坚持传统的一面，而促使这两者共存的原因之一就是幻想元素的运用。根据休姆的分析法，幻想有三大主要功能——增强、削弱和对比（83）。通过揭示想象版的生活与现实世界的差异，幻想强化了情节的推进，并加剧了主题冲突的效果。幻想和现实对峙之时，便是人物的顿悟时刻，而化解通常是通过高潮冲突之后产生的新认知来表述的。

在她大部分的作品中，幻想元素的应用达到了她预设的目的，即探索并评判现实的本质。她的幻想世界中的两大特征——人物对真理和爱情的诚挚追求，以及他们对残酷现实表现出的义愤——是她能够跻身于二十世纪严肃作家队列的原因之一。

第一章

导论：曼斯菲尔德与幻想

由于人们对凯瑟琳·曼斯菲尔德小说艺术的某些领域探研不足，她经常被不公正地视为边缘作家。从她青涩的少年习作到 1923 年去世前所著的较为成熟的作品中，几乎都可以找到运用幻想元素的例子，她的这一作品特色也正是尚待探索的研究领域之一。尽管狂热的追崇者和苛刻的评论家对她的评价呈现两极分化，他们却似乎一致认为她的艺术本质是神秘的，往往无法定义。其中，马文·马格拉纳（Marvin Magalaner）选择了"凯瑟琳·曼斯菲尔德之谜"（"The Enigma of Katherine Mansfield"）作为他的评著《凯瑟琳·曼斯菲尔德小说论》第一章的标题。与他不谋而合，克莱尔·汉森（Clare Hanson）如此描述了曼斯菲尔德的作品："充满隐喻、难以捉摸"（"Introduction" 9）。然而，他们二人都未能大胆解读出幻想的持续运用是曼斯菲尔德捉摸不定的写作风格的一个组成部分，更不必说小说创作技巧了。

赫伯特·戈尔德是早期试图从幻想的本质和作用的角度来定义幻想与短篇小说艺术之间的关系的评论家之一。他认为幻想是"对生活可能性的梦想，它使人带有人性"（450）。他进一步指出，"尽管如此，作家们仍然愿意把他们的（幻想）魔力当作信仰、法律概念、社会愿景的过滤器"（451）。他认为当幻想成功地运用于一件艺术作品中时，它"似乎比对日常生活的恐惧显得更确凿，更真实"，就像"故事"总比"历史""更为真实、更具哲理"（451—452）。纳丁·戈迪默的观点则稍有不同。她坚持认为"幻想仅仅是一种角度的变化"和"一个观察终极现实的更广阔视角"（459—460）。她通过一个有趣的比喻进一步阐明了她的观点：

如同透过玻璃杯底部看到的图案那样，幻想是一种会变化、融合、浮现、消失的东西。当你透过玻璃杯往下看的那一刻，它是真实的；但是同样的幻象并不会改变你所看到的一切，那是始终如一地贯穿在一个人的整体意识里的。（460）

凯瑟琳·休姆在《幻想和模拟》（*Fantasy and Mimesis*）一书中反对将模拟现实的文学和幻想文学作生硬的划分，她认为文学作品都是两种驱动力的结合体。其中之一是模拟——"渴望以逼真的方式模拟、描述能让人感同身受的事件、人物、情景和物体"。另一个驱动力则是幻想——"出于无聊、好玩、憧憬、对所缺之物的渴望……而想要改变现状和现实的欲望"（20）。因此，她的定义更具包容性："**幻想是对任何公认的现实的背离**，这是文学固有的一种驱动力，它的表现形式多种多样，从怪物到隐喻不等。"（21）

无论他们的定义相差多远，他们都一致认为幻想既是在表达对现实的不满，也是在表达对处理现实的传统方法的不满。它是一个相对新颖、更加自由的探索生命终极真理的方法。曼斯菲尔德在援引黑格尔的话作以下评述时，一定是凭直觉领悟到这一点的：

为什么思维和存在必须处于两个不同层面？为什么黑格尔尝试将主观过程转化为客观世界的进程一定行不通？"通过存在之外的其他途径抵达存在，是思维的特殊艺术和目标。"也就是说，现实不可能成为理想，也不可能成为梦想；艺术家的职责不是磨利斧子，试图把他的人生愿景强加于客观世界。艺术家不是试图调解客观存在和个人愿景之间的矛盾，而是试图在这个世界里创造出自己的世界。（*Journal* 273）

我们只要稍加调整，便可以将上述观点看作曼斯菲尔德谦逊的艺术宣言，它将愿景和存在二者并列为同一现实的两种不同视角。以幻想的方式抵达现实，也意味着获取了现实存在范围之外的相对行动自由。就她的小说创作艺术而言，幻象世界或幻想世界往往以白日梦和角色扮演的形式出现，此二者都与想要逃避公认的"现实"的内心驱动力有关。

对曼斯菲尔德来说，幻想不仅是她小说的整体特征，而且还是体现她哲学姿态的一个侧面。在其小说框架内研究幻想的应用，是把握她的艺术原则以及她对人性看法的途径之一。但不幸的是，自她去世以后，这个问题在漫长的几十年里一直没有得到应有的关注。许多研究她的评论家一直忙于挖掘她的传记资料，解析她的作品与生活中已知事件的联系。比较研究领域出版了不少论著，主要研考契诃夫和法国象征主义对她创作艺术的影响。有几本著作试图将其写作中的某些特质剥离开来，偶尔也触及幻想的应用。例如，安德鲁·格尔（Andrew Gurr）所著的《流亡作家》（*Writers in Exile*）追溯了曼斯菲尔德的部分人生经历，正是这些经历促成了她笔下的人物拥有白日梦和角色扮演的特点。但从本质上来说，这本书是在研究流亡对作家群体的总体影响。凯特·富布鲁克（Kate Fullbrook）的《凯瑟琳·曼斯菲尔德》（*Katherine Mansfield*）一书探索了碎片化自我和二**重身**主题，该主题是曼斯菲尔德幻想世界的一个组成部分。尽管如此，富布鲁克的研究重点还是在探索曼斯菲尔德的女权主义思想基础和她不断穿越性别边界的尝试，富布鲁克想在两者之间找到一种认同关系。

在为数不多的将幻想作为主要关注点的研究中，切丽·汉金（Cherry Hankin）所著的《凯瑟琳·曼斯菲尔德作品中的幻想和结局感》（"Fantasy and the Sense of an Ending in the Work of Katherine Mansfield"）一文和《凯瑟琳·曼斯菲尔德和她的自白体故事》（*Katherine Mansfield and Her Confessional Stories*）一书的研究范围最为宽泛。尤其是后者，比较系统地考察了曼斯菲尔德的整体作品，并依据她本人的情感经历追溯了其作品的发展过程。在这部心理传记著作中，汉金描绘并分析了曼斯菲尔德的情感生活和她小说中幻想元素的平行发展，特别强调她"用她自己的梦想和失望作为小说的素材"，并"利用所有的艺术资源来伪装、疏隔、塑造她的主题"（*Confessional Stories X*）。

本文在一定程度上借鉴了汉金的研究，特别是在幻想的运用与曼斯菲尔德小说主题模式之间的联系上。不同的是，我将幻想的研究扩展到了小说技巧的范畴，曼斯菲尔德正是因此而脱颖成为一名伟大的作家，成功"协助英语短篇小说走向成人的自由世界"（Bates 124）。本文从人物塑造的角度分析了幻想的功能。由于曼斯菲尔德既相信又怀疑一个统一自我的存在可能性，她笔下的人物陷入了困境。他们在两种欲念间困顿挣扎：既沉湎于习惯性的角色扮演，又渴望从众多虚假的"自我"中区分出一个真实"自我"，并实现这个真实"自我"。曼斯菲尔德对他们多重经历的描绘，为读者提供了多重视角来探究他们的内心世界。因此，幻想的使用有助于展现人物心理的复杂性。

本文还从意象模式、象征意义等方面对幻想元素进行了探讨。曼斯菲尔德一再反对使用分析方法，倾向于通过创意写作中的暗示来获取启示。她的幻想世界由一系列充满联想意义的意象组成。虽然其早期作品主要集中在一个"梦幻人物"身上，但她后期小说的焦点转移到了用形象表述的自然世界。通过在幻想境界中展示这样的意象和象征，曼斯菲尔德揭示了生活中普遍存在争议的一面：人类对真爱和艺术之美难以遏制的渴望，以及交织而来的当渴望无法满足时的绝望。

根据休姆的定义，幻想有三个基本功能：增强、削弱和对比。这三个功能在曼斯菲尔德的小说中都显而易见。因此，本文还旨在探讨幻想对曼斯菲尔德叙事结构的影响。幻想的这三个功能都以不同的方式揭示了它与现实的差异以及导致的冲突，从而强化了情节发展，增强了主题冲突的效果。高潮冲突通常引入了隐含的化解，因为人物在某个顿悟的时刻意识到了梦想在改变现实方面的无能为力，从而获得了对生活的新认知。

曼斯菲尔德小说中幻想元素的重复出现并不是偶然的。自她早逝以后，浮现的大量传记资料揭示了她生命中的几个突出方面，可以拿来解释她沉迷于梦幻的原因。本章的其余部分会探讨其中一些方面。

凯瑟琳·曼斯菲尔德于1888年出生在新西兰惠灵顿，原名凯瑟琳·布尚（Kathleen Beauchamp）。孩童时期，她生活在一个物质生活丰裕，但情感生活相对匮乏的家庭环境之中。她觉得自己不如兄弟姐妹受疼爱，因为她出生时全家都期待着一个男孩和家族继承人。她早熟且敏感，从小就感受到一种男性占优势的压迫和威胁。这种感觉首先来源于她个性专横的父亲，而后也来自她那个天生就能吸引全家人关注的唯一的弟弟莱斯利。除了祖母，她没有其他人可以谈心，所以她变成了一个"喜怒无常、充满忿恨""目光犀利"的女孩（Alpers 13）。小凯思（曼斯菲尔德年幼时的乳名）作为一个孤独者，在自己的幻想王国中寻求着慰藉。

后来，曼斯菲尔德在她的一些作品，尤其是少年习作中，创造出一些温柔的父母亲形象，借此重新塑造了她孩童时期所匮乏的充满爱意的家庭氛围。根据汉金所述，《他的梦中母亲》（"His Ideal"）是曼斯菲尔德现存最早的作品，其核心人物是一个柔弱的、捉摸不定的替身母亲形象。一直到年轻的主人公身陷病榻时，这位替身母亲才对他显现。她的出现毋庸置疑地让人产生关于纯洁的联想：

> 她身材高挑，着一件白色长袍，如月光般闪闪发亮。她那白皙的颈脖裸露在外……她俯视着他，脸上充满温柔和怜悯。啊！他不知情，他这可怜的小孩，并不知情，张着双臂要她抱，要她安慰，要她把自己搂在怀里。（Hankin *Confessional Stories* 8）

然而这个恍若天仙的女人拒绝走出幻想的领地。她消失了，留下这个"非常非常疲惫的"孩子对她苦苦思念。当她最终回应他的呼唤归来时，他已年迈，感觉到"他所有的悲伤、眼泪和痛苦都消失在了过去"（9）。他栖息在她温柔的臂弯里，这时才意识到她的名字是死神。

一年之后的1904年，曼斯菲尔德创作了《我的盆栽》（"My Potplant"），文中再现了主人公与一位异常迷人但却捉摸不定的母亲形象相遇的模式，这一次，这位母亲是一个林中女子。然而在这篇小说中，主人公承认幻想不可能实现，从而放弃了追求。正如小说结尾所述，她决定"加入队伍中去，与大千世界抗争"（Hankin *Confessional Stories* 14）。

曼斯菲尔德偶尔会把童年幻想沿用到她一些更为成熟的作品中。例如，《家庭女教师》（"The Little Governess"）中所描述的贫穷女教师的慕尼黑历险之旅，显然基于曼斯菲尔德自己对火车上遇见的一位旅行者的幻想。想象中的慈爱爷爷，最终变成了一个披着伪装的性侵犯者，这位家庭女教师对于真实亲情的幻想，被现实无情地粉碎了。

曼斯菲尔德在幻梦中寻找替代品的习惯并没有随着她童年的消逝而消失。事实上，她的少年和短暂的成年经历在不断地扩展着她的幻想能力。在她的后期作品中，幻想的重复出现很大程度上是她一生中众多对立力量相互作用的结果，首当其冲的是她对艺术自由的渴望以及如影随形的对放逐的恐惧。安德鲁·格尔在分析了流亡作家的状态之后，得出了以下见解：

> 流亡艺术家就像系在拔河绳子中间的布带，它标志着两股剑拔弩张的力量间的静止点。其中一股力量是他自己的个性，个性使他成为艺术家……而另一股力量是未知的牵引力，是流亡者丢失了源自社会归属感的身份认同而产生的茫然恐惧。艺术家对社会的反抗使他知悉自己的个性；而对自己的放逐则使他丢失了自己的个性。如果绳子两头的力量势均力敌，布带下的绳子会颤动但不会挪移。同样，艺术家会朝着一个方向努力，去实现他的个人愿景，但却会发现无法靠近它，因为对面有来自社会身份的反牵引力。社会身份塑造了艺术家的个性，没有它，他便没有任何身份，也就没有任何个性。（33）

这正是凯瑟琳·曼斯菲尔德在她那短暂的创作生涯中的处境。

她出生时，新西兰作为一个单独的英国殖民地，还不到五十年历史，那里的大多数居民仍视英国为他们的"家园"。布尚家族所属的商人阶层是当时社会的主导力量，中产阶级价值观念是评判一个人社会成就的准则。作为艺术家，曼斯菲尔德远比作为女人成熟得早，这与惠灵顿社会发展的步伐不相适宜，因为当时的物质发展相当迅速，而文化进步相对缓慢。1906 年末，当她在伦敦皇后学院接受三年教育之后被催促返家时，她觉得乏味的惠灵顿生活是场彻头彻尾的噩梦。她一直担心自己年轻的艺术天赋会被扼杀在这片不能激发和鼓励灵感的土地上。她写于 1907 年 10 月 21 日的一则日记很能说明她当时的心情：

> 待在自己的房间里，我感觉好像是在伦敦。在伦敦呀！就连写这个词都让我觉得自己忍不住要流泪。对一件事爱得如此深沉难道不可怕吗？我根本不在乎男人，我在乎的是**伦敦**。那才叫生活啊……我渴望和比我强的人们待在一起。我到底是怎么了？我真是个虚荣至极的无名小卒吗？我不知道……但我实在很不开心。这就是我的感受。我不开心到了期望死去的地步——但是，我还**丁点儿**都没活过就死了，这也未免太疯狂了。（21）

这是微弱却愤怒的呼唤艺术自由的声音，是害怕被淹没在浩瀚的中产阶级常规生活的海洋中的声音。后来，在同一则日记中，曼斯菲尔德开始幻想在一个具有优越文化环境的社会中的生活：

> 我喜欢显得……全然从容自在，意识到自己的重要性。这在我看来，就是不受限制的、愉悦的、心态开放的。我喜欢显得有点儿高傲，见过**大世面**，成为众人关注的焦点。（22）

但她年轻时的幻想并未实现，因为伦敦迟迟未能赏识她的价值。她的第一部小说集《在德国公寓里》（*In a German Pension*，1911）是一系列情感旋风的产物，并没有引起读者的热烈反响，只招来了诸如"精明的观察者"之类的评价（Alpers 129）。第二年，当她开始和约翰·米德尔顿·莫里（John Middleton Murry）同居时，她的职业生涯发生了一点转变。莫里是一位初出茅庐的评论家和编辑，在他的小杂志《韵律》（*Rhythm*）和奥拉基（A. P. Orage）的《新时代期刊》（*New Age*）之间，曼斯菲尔德找到了一个可以展示自己艺术天赋的空间。

然而莫里两口子依旧游走在伦敦文学精英阶层的边缘。我们可以从以下两个事实中看出他们不属于波希米亚圈子的主流。首先，正如格尔所指出的那样，他们的大多数亲密友人本身都是流亡者（39）。例如曼斯菲尔德曾经的良师益友碧娅翠丝·哈斯汀（Beatrice Hasting）来自南非；她的闺蜜碧娅翠丝·康贝尔（Beatrice Compbell）来自爱尔兰；好友寇特良斯基（Koteliansky）是俄罗斯人；曾经和她关系很亲密的弗里达·劳伦斯（Frieda Lawrence）也被她的祖国德国放逐。其次，布卢姆斯伯里圈子里的人从未平等地看待过他们的社会地位。例如，弗吉尼亚·伍尔芙在她 1917 年 10 月 11 日的日记中，用寥寥几笔提及了她和曼斯菲尔德的第一次会面。她把曼斯菲尔德描述成"普通的""廉价的""像只在街上徘徊的狸猫"那样带着一股气味（*Diary Vol. I* 58）。这股尖酸刻薄后来有所和缓，因为伍尔芙们发现了曼斯菲尔德隐藏于表象之下的闪光才华。即便如此，他们之间的阶级藩篱仍然存在着。在伍尔芙们眼中，莫里两口子仍被归在不入流的文人堆里。从莫里的自传《两个世界之间》（*Between Two Worlds*）中，我们可以感觉到这种排斥是相互的，因为曼斯菲尔德也觉得待在时尚的伦敦文学沙龙里颇不自在：

> 那是个愚蠢的、不真实的夜晚：华丽的房间、靓丽的人们、精美的咖啡，还有银罐装的香烟，都笼罩着梅雷迪斯小说里的那股虚假气氛……我很难受。我和"迷人的"女人们没什么话好讲，我觉得自己就像混迹于虎群中的一只猫。（290）

曼斯菲尔德成功地把这些印象转化到了她的一些小说之中。《幸福》（"Bliss"）中自命不凡、肤浅的诺曼·奈特一家和《时髦的婚姻》（"Marriage A La Mode"）中伊莎贝尔喧闹的艺术家朋友们，都明显地反映出她所结识的伦敦波希米亚文人们的生活方式。在这副坚硬的尊严面具背后，不难察觉到根植于这个"在伦敦花园中漫步""或许准予参观，但不可逗留"的"小殖民地居民"身上的自卑情结所留下的痕迹（*Journal* 157）。她的声音异常孤独且犹疑，她的经济窘境进一步阻碍了她"与社会上轻浮、无忧无虑的那群人混在一起"（Hormasji 48）。

这就是曼斯菲尔德在 1908—1923 年间的处境。她不得不告别惠灵顿，因为它与她的性情不符。她心甘情愿地在欧洲，尤其在英国，流放了十四年之久，但这并未能消除她作为外乡人的感受。正如西尔维娅·伯克曼（Sylvia Berkman）在她那部发人深省的曼斯菲尔德评传中所示："她挣脱了祖国的束缚，却发现给予她希望和信仰的那个国家碎裂了。她回不去了，她已错过返回的时机。她必须在自己的内心寻找或创造一个新世界。"（146）

曼斯菲尔德很快就创造出这个"内心世界"。她那些有关新西兰的小说被公认为是所有作品中的精品，它们是她在现实世界中经受的孤独和幻灭所结出的果实。许多评论家过分强调了她弟弟的死亡对于她决定书写他们的共同家园所起的作用。她那"拂去我同胞身上的迷雾，让人们看见他们"（*Letters* 75）的想法，绝不是一时的任性冲动。她描绘得如此美丽而浪漫的新西兰已不再是她 1908 年离去时的那片土地，而是她儿时幻想的延续。这片土地已远非现实世界的任何破坏性力量所能及，它的丑陋之处已被时空的安全距离所模糊。

促成幻想场景在小说中一再出现的第二种对立力量，是曼斯菲尔德分裂的情感生活。它就像钟摆一样，不断地在对和谐婚姻生活的渴望和对同性恋女友的依恋之间摇摆不定。曼斯菲尔德对男人的态度从一开始就是矛盾的。她对男性的不满，淋漓尽致地显现在了诸如男人过度的性需求以及由此导致的女人分娩创伤的小说主题上。早在 1907 年，她就开始表现出同性恋的倾向，与两个惠灵顿女孩有过一段炙热的情史。这些青少年轶事只是她与约翰·米德尔顿·莫里和艾达·康斯坦斯·贝克（Ida Constance Baker）之间微妙的三角关系的前奏，这段三角关系在她的成年生活中持续了十一年之久。曼斯菲尔德的婚姻绝不是平静的，习惯性的小题大做使得她的情感生活每时每刻都处于危机之中。最初由于不同的作息习惯和相处时彼此的压抑感，后来则是由于她的病情，她必须与莫里暂时分离，她的情绪在炙热的爱和同样强烈的恨之间辗转反复。她将他们的情感冲突归咎于他们生活中的角色逆转：

我们曾经是彼此的**孩子**，公开承认的孩子，彼此无话不谈，平等地依赖着对方。在此之前，我一直是男人，他一直是女人，而且从未有人要求他付出真正的努力。他从来没有真正"支持"过我。后来，我的病越来越糟，它把我变成了一个女人……他不可思议地承受住了。（*Scrapbook* 147−148）

很显然，曼斯菲尔德和莫里的关系中的悲剧元素不过是曼斯菲尔德心智上的自我和肉体上的自我相互冲突的结果。她的心智一直是精力充沛、充满阳刚之气的，但她的病却使她的肉体变成了一个脆弱而依赖人的女人。当莫里未能作出相应的改变时，两人的关系就进一步恶化了。

在他们的感情抑郁期发作时，艾达·康斯坦斯·贝克——又名莱斯利·摩尔（Leslie Moore）——就被很顺手地招呼来"用这个来对付那个"（Hankin *Confessional Stories* 166）。但曼斯菲尔德对莱斯利·摩尔的需求只是阶段性的，她的日记和信件中充斥着轻蔑的词语，将她们的关系形容为"可以想象得到的最深切的仇敌"（*Journal* 153）。她对莱斯利·摩尔的种种非难很难简单地解释为她在小题大做，或者是她在借此向莫里保证他是她的首选，尽管莱斯利·摩尔在她的《记忆》一书中想要我们如此相信（234，236）。摩尔才智上的局限性注定了她无法成为曼斯菲尔德文学交流上旗鼓相当的伴侣，更为重要的是，她那毫不质疑的忠诚反而激怒了曼斯菲尔德，因为这让她想起了莫里的不足。

曼斯菲尔德在经历了与男女两性的爱情之后，发现爱情并不能使她满足，因而不得不再次折返内心，在幻想中构建理想的爱情王国。她于1913年创作的《一件稚气但十分自然的事》（"Something Childish But Very Natural"）反映了她早期对爱情的一些想法，当时她与莫里的生活依然很幸福。它讲述的是两个年轻恋人亨利和埃德娜的故事，他们在通勤列车上相遇并坠入爱河。但埃德娜因为担心他们的关系"会全然改变"、他们"不再是孩童了"，而不愿与亨利有任何肉体接触（*Something Childish and Other Stories* 145）。女主人公，或者更确切地说是曼斯菲尔德自己，相信只要清白保持完好，爱情便能永恒。在这个故事中，曼斯菲尔德已经暗示了日常亲昵行为的破坏性影响，因为埃德娜在故事结尾并未出现在他们计划共同生活的小房子里。

在曼斯菲尔德后来的小说中，当她作为女人和艺术家的角色同时走向成熟时，这种理想化的、天真无邪的爱情模式逐渐消失，她笔下的一些陷入了情感危机的人物，开始通过另一种幻想形式来寻求慰藉。她们渴望基于相互理解和情感的婚姻，如《序曲》（"Prelude"）中的琳达·伯纳尔。她们也渴望与同性分享真实情感，尽管收效甚微；她们有时就像《幸福》中的伯莎·杨那样，在不同的场合里改变自己的性角色，只是她们不再坚持用幻梦来代替现实。这种相对的独立令她们有了一定程度上的自由，可以在主观愿景世界和客观现实之间游移行走。

除了这些伴随曼斯菲尔德一生的双向牵引力之外，第一次世界大战也是她的作品"转向内心世界"的主要原因。战争初期，莫里夫妇仍然在他们自给自足的文字世界中漫游，未受局势干扰，他们天真地相信"战争……不是**为了**什么事儿——什么重要的事儿"（Murry *Between the Two Worlds* 299）。但曼斯菲尔德很快就震惊地意识到了战争对她个人的影响。首先，大轰炸使她在巴黎滞留了三个星期，这期间她的肺病严重恶化。其次，她唯一的弟弟莱斯利以及莫里的许多朋友都未能从战场生还。莫里夫妇不能再装出一副漠不关心的样子了，他们开始质疑战争的意义。实际上，曼斯菲尔德对弗吉尼亚·伍尔芙在作品中对战争只字不提的冷漠做法感到愤慨（*Letters to Murry* 381）。

随着战争的爆发，公认的真理在他们的面前崩塌，没有任何东西可以填补这个空白；旧的价值体系分崩离析，而新的价值体系尚未出现。如果说放逐带来的恐惧和情感危机已经给曼斯菲尔德对人性的整体信心罩上了质疑的阴影，那么战争就彻底粉碎了她对整个世界的看法，留下她独自在黑暗中探索着自己的道路。正如伯克曼所指出的那样，共同信念的衰败会导致：

> 探索者被驱赶至自己的内心，在碎片中构建自己的愿景世界。于是，我们绽开了个体表达之花，它由个体经验所产生的个体气质所塑造，并由个体气质和个体经验来检验其真伪。（150）

如果还有真理存在的话，那么现在就必须从新的角度来探求了。于是，一个以个人愿景和心声来探索真理的新视角，在曼斯菲尔德的小说世界中以幻想的形式应运而生了。

第二章

幻想与人物塑造

在《幻想和模拟》（*Fantasy and Mimesis*）一书中，凯瑟琳·休姆根据幻想与情节及人物塑造之间的不同联系将其分成了三大类。根据她的说法，第一类是"基于行动的幻想"，在这种幻想中，"逃离现实的愿望产生了行动"。第二类是"基于人物的幻想"，它通常采用的形式是一个"非人类叙述者"讲述的故事。第三类则是"基于想法的幻想"，它的中心是一个不引发人物行为、但可能对其产生影响的奇幻想法（159—162）。仔细阅读凯瑟琳·曼斯菲尔德的作品，我们可以看出：她对幻想的运用有时并不受休姆这几个分类的限制，尤其是当她将幻想作为一种人物塑造的辅助手段时。她的大多数小说中的场景都是严格仿制现实的，尽管她的人物存在于幻想的世界中，但他们显然不是神话人物，他们的梦境很少会扩展到行动领域。这实际上就排除了与休姆的前两个分类的任何关联。的确，曼斯菲尔德小说中的大部分主人公都沉溺于幻想之中，但幻想却并不一定改变他们的生活方式，也不一定会严重影响到他们与其他人的关系。因此，人物形象的塑造不是取决于他们的行为而是取决于他们的思维过程。

曼斯菲尔德诉诸角色扮演和白日梦这两种基本的、相互关联的幻想形式来塑造她的人物，这两种形式都遵循了她的"自我"概念。在一部从女性主义角度研究曼斯菲尔德的著作中，凯特·富布鲁克注意到了曼斯菲尔德摇摆不定的态度——对于是否存在着一个统一的自我，她既相信又心存疑虑。曼斯菲尔德在日记中也重申了"深信但却抗拒有持续存在的自我，这个自我有可能从角色、面具和碎片中解脱出来，成为纯粹的存在"（Fullbrook 19）。曼斯菲尔德在 1920 年 4 月底的一则日记中戏谑地提出了对自我本质的追问：

　　忠于自我！哪个自我？众多自我——真的看起来有——千百个自我中的哪一个？在那些复杂的、压抑的、回应的、震荡的、反省的思考过程中，有时候我觉得自己不过是个在某家没有老板的旅馆里工作的小职员，所有的任务就是录入房客姓名，然后把钥匙交给那些自作主张的客人。(205)

　　曼斯菲尔德认识到人类心理中多个自我的存在，但同时她也并未对追求一个持续的、一致的自我而陷入彻底的绝望。她将文学作品中"急切渴求自白"的现象归咎于以下的原因：

　　……有迹象表明我们比以往任何时候都渴望弄清楚什么是独特的自我，并试图遵循独特的自我准则生活。人类必须是自由的（此句原文为德语——引者注）——自由、解脱羁绊、独立存在。我们执着而神秘地相信着一个持续而永恒的自我的存在……不为后天得来的和舍弃的东西所动。这个信念难道就不能在枯叶和腐泥中扎出一把绿色的长矛，让一个鳞状花蕾穿过多年的黑暗破土而出，直至某一天光发现了它，让它自由绽放——我们活了——我们在地球上为属于自己的那一刻而盛开怒放？毕竟，我们是为了这一刻而活的……(*Journal* 205)

　　这种发现自我的"开花"时刻被后来的作家如詹姆斯·乔伊斯和弗吉尼亚·伍尔芙称为"顿悟"和"存在时刻"。对曼斯菲尔德而言，这种时刻是无限微小且转瞬即逝的，而面对一个支离破碎的自我时所产生的困惑状态则是普遍的、挥之不去的。在自我是"多重、变换、非持续性的"和"无本质"的情况下，身份就成了一个相对脆弱的术语（Fullbrook 17）。由于多重自我中的每一个自我都是难以捉摸和转瞬即逝的，因此应该人为地构建一个相对具体和一致的形象，以发挥人的社会功能并避免使其陷入彻底碎片化的境遇。曼斯菲尔德在写作生涯的初期就意识到了一个公众自我（也就是她所说的"面具"）存在的必要性。她一再告诫丈夫莫里，即使独处时也不可放下这副面具（*Letters to Murry* 94）。

这种自我的概念既解释了她作品中的许多角色为何沉迷于角色扮演的原因，也阐明了她通过揭示角色冲突来塑造人物形象的创作方法。若用"真"和"假"这样的标签来分析这些在她的幻想世界里出现的分裂的自我，那就未免过于简单化了，因为每一个自我都同样体现并忠于人物性格，都反映出该人物的某个侧面（哪怕是微不足道的），并有助于塑造他的整体存在。

与托马斯·哈代笔下的裘德和尤斯塔西娅不同，曼斯菲尔德塑造的男女主人公通常并不会感受到在社会环境中错位的**剧烈**疼痛。他们也不似乔治·艾略特在《亚当·比德》（*Adam Bede*）中塑造的人物黛娜·莫里斯那样，在追求宗教或道德真理时与自己的灵魂苦苦博弈。他们最根本的不快乐或失望通常源自他们意识到了众多自我之间的矛盾冲突，或者自己的直觉天性与预期的社会功能之间的矛盾。因此，他们的战争不是针对居心险恶的上帝或者卑鄙的社会，他们抗争的那个敌人只是他们自身；他们的战争并不发生在广阔的自然世界，而是在狭小的人类心灵；他们作战时并不借助于一系列的外在动作，而是通过对个人意识的逐渐揭示。由于曼斯菲尔德的文学意图显然集中在心理活动的探索上，因此情节注定不能成为塑造人物的有效手段。通过揭示外在危机来塑造人物的传统写作方式必须由一种新方法取代。

曼斯菲尔德很快就会发现这种新方法。她在大部分作品中引入了幻想的技巧，不仅通过以白日梦的形式揭示其内心危机来探讨人物内心世界，同时也通过他们所扮演的不同角色来探索他们不同的人生视角。在他们寻求"根本"自我的过程中，顿悟时刻，或者说洞察时刻，就成为醍醐灌顶的庄严时刻。但是正如伊莲·肖瓦尔特（Elaine Showalter）在《他们自己的文学》（*A Literature of Their Own* 247）一书中断言的那样，这同时也是一个恐怖和"崩溃"的时刻，因为破译"自我"神话，也就意味着对它失去信念。这些一闪而过的洞察或启示时刻以及它们暗含的矛盾，后来都成了曼斯菲尔德人物塑造过程中的聚焦点。

曼斯菲尔德的许多作品中的主人公都是自我放纵的角色扮演家。他们喜欢变戏法似的召唤出自己诸多的幻想世界，每个世界里都居住着一个具有假定人格的人，他们在这个世界里可以逃避不愉快的现实，并且隐喻性地实现他们的秘密心愿。《家庭女教师》中那个多愁善感的女主人公就是这个庞大群体中的一员，这篇小说带着丝丝缕缕作者自身与弗朗西斯·卡科（Francis Carco）在短暂的浪漫史之后感受到的"羞辱和自责的痛苦情绪"（Hankin *Confessional Stories* 97—98）。

初读《家庭女教师》，你会认为它是个老掉牙的天真客游历海外的故事，而女主人公只是曼斯菲尔德众多的"无法区分何为真相何为如意梦想"的可悲人物中的一员（Hankin 98）。然而再次阅读时，就会发现掩藏于表层之下的更深的真相。曼斯菲尔德通过描绘家庭女教师所扮演的不同角色及其角色之间必然导致的冲突，从而塑造出一个微妙而复杂的人物。这个人物表面上的天真其实只是为了逃避成人世界的责任而作出的姿态，同时也是为了掩饰她渴望获得来自男性的爱和保护的心愿。这种角色扮演综合征的第一个症状，就是女主人公一直萎缩在漫长的童年茧壳之中。这种状态被纳瑞曼·霍马斯基（Nariman Hormasji）描述为时而"接近神经官能症"的"巨婴化行为"（89）。

在家庭教师管理局的一次会面中——这只是正剧开始之前的一个场景，女教师就已经开始显露出对他人超乎寻常的依赖感。她以一种孩子气的、毫不置疑的态度听取了主管女士提供的信息。当去往德国的长途旅行开始时，她毫不费力地进入了一个渴望得到父母关爱的孩童角色：

> 在女客舱里过得很好。女服务员真好，替她换了钱，还帮她把脚裹在毯子里。她躺在一张有粉红小碎花的硬沙发上，看着其他乘客友善而自然地把帽子别在靠枕上，脱下靴子和裙子，打开衣柜归整她们窸窣作响的神秘小包裹，系好头纱之后躺了下来。突，突，突，轮船稳稳地驶动了。女服务员拉下绿色的罩子遮住了灯光，在炉子旁边坐下，裙子翻到膝盖之上，腿上放着一样长长的织了一半的东西。"我好喜欢旅行啊。"家庭女教师心想。她微笑着臣服在轮船温暖的摇晃之中。（*Bliss and Other Stories* 240）

在这里，这个无名的家庭女教师模拟着在父母庇护下外出旅行的情景，借此回避人生进入成年期的第一次旅程的严肃性。在她的幻想中，她显然把女服务员的日常工作解读成母爱的象征。舒适的客舱让她想起了摇篮，就连她选择休息的沙发也是粉色的，使人联想到梦境。她对周围琐事的关注显示出一个孩子的好奇心（尽管是假装的），因为只有孩子才会如此不加质疑地观察世界。

船舶靠岸之后，家庭女教师仍然保持她的婴化行为，她一丝不苟地按照家庭教师管理局那位女士给的建议行事——"一开始最好要对人怀有戒心，不可相信他们"（239）。当她走出船舱时，她变得过度戒备。搬运工走近并拉住她的行李时，她匆忙地断定他是个"劫匪"（241）。后来，她再次扮演了一个小女孩的角色，无视成人世界的规则，故意拒绝向铁路搬运工和酒店服务员支付其应得的小费。但即使假装是个孩子，她也无法使自己免于成人世界的惩罚——在以上这两件事上，她就像许多维多利亚时期犯错的女主人公一样，因为违逆了成人世界的法规而受到了惩处。

当小说进展到中间时，家庭女教师的角色从一个毫无质疑能力的孩子转变成了一个具有自我意识的年轻女性，这表明曼斯菲尔德在试图增强人物形象的复杂性。不同角色之间的转换时刻也正是它们产生冲突的时刻，作者由此捕捉到并随后向读者传达了家庭女教师身上远比一个单纯的"游历海外的天真客"要微妙得多的"根本"特性。例如当女教师第一眼看到她的旅伴——她幻想中的祖父时，她立刻显露出对他的兴趣，而这种兴趣并非全然与性无关：

作为一个老头儿，他可是非常干净整洁的。黑领带上别着一枚珍珠别针，小拇指上戴着一枚镶着暗红色宝石的戒指，双排扣外套的口袋里露出一角白丝手帕。总之，他整体看起来很英俊。（246）

她发现了他身体的吸引力之后，才开始调整自己的态度——她的角色开始由孩童让位给年轻女人。当她意识到老人在关注自己时，她"透过长长的睫毛偷看着他"（246），"对他露出酒窝"（252），"她面泛桃红，红晕慢慢扩散到双颊，衬得她的蓝眼睛看起来几乎是黑色的"（246）。她对自己青春魅力的戏剧化演绎听起来完全是情绪泛滥的：

> 唉！一个小小的家庭女教师拥有一头让人联想起橘子、金盏花、杏子、玳瑁猫和香槟酒的头发，真是太悲惨了！即使丑陋的深色服饰也不能遮掩她的柔美。（247）

她对他的关注不断作出回应，从而进一步激发了他的兴趣。她很快就使他成为自己的知己，对他不无风情地倾诉着自己的生平故事。当他犹犹疑疑地建议他们可否一起"度个小假"时，她又暧昧地回答说不能答应他，因为她是"一个人"（249）。在慕尼黑旅行期间，她允许他挽着她的胳膊，走在她近旁，两人合用一把伞。她的言谈举止与一个陶醉于爱的梦境的女人别无二致。这位家庭女教师似乎在害怕自己的第一次情感体验，因此不断地传唤着一个天真的"孩子"的角色，来为自己作为年轻女人的风骚行为做辩护。就像她以渴望双亲庇护为幌子来遮掩她那刚刚苏醒的性渴望一样，她也把他那多情的关注幻想成是祖父式的关爱。以下这段独白就是她自圆其说的一个例子：

> **也许**（强调为引者所加）他脸颊和嘴唇上的红晕是出于一股怒气，为如此年轻柔弱的一位女子竟然在夜间无人守护独自旅行而感到愤怒。谁知道他有没有以他多愁善感的德国风格小声嘀咕："**是的，这是个悲剧**（此句原文为德语——引者注）！上帝啊，要是我是这孩子的爷爷多好！"（247）

同样，她对自己的风骚也颇不以为然，认为这只是对他的草莓、冰淇淋和慕尼黑之旅的谢意而已。随着对老人的依恋加增，"爷爷"和"神仙祖父"这样的词出现得愈加频繁。但不幸的是，那个"祖父"只是她的幻想产物。在他那个丑陋的公寓里，当他将"那僵硬的老态龙钟的身躯紧紧贴着她"（259）并强行索取了她的初吻时，幻想的世界在她面前消失了，她唯一能说出来的一句话是："这是个梦！这不是真的！"（259）汉金指出了故事的反讽之处——"像这个小家庭女教师一样需要学那么多东西的人，是完全没有资格开始教书育人的生涯的"（*Confessional Stories* 99）。但这个故事还有另外一层反讽意义：骗人的面纱被确立为现实的真面目，而赤裸的真相却是在梦幻般的模糊境界里呈现的。

当两个分裂的自我最终进入对峙时，家庭女教师的危机时刻来临了。她扮演的孩童角色使她陷入了一种依赖状态，在这种状态下她可以向人索取关注和关照，而不必为此承担相应的责任。然而，她的另一个自我——一个年轻的渐渐成熟的女人角色，却迫使她不得不面对自己的情感冒险所带来的后果。由于这两个角色都代表了小家庭女教师身上的复杂人性的一个侧面，它们之间的不可协调性使得人物的心理世界变得更为丰富。

F. M. 佩瑞（F. M. Perry）是与曼斯菲尔德同时代的评论家之一，他在《短篇小说的写作艺术》（*The Art of Story-writing*）一书中提到：曼斯菲尔德最成功的作品是那些将人物"置于相互回应关系之中"的小说（213）。二十五年后，西尔维娅·伯克曼也对曼斯菲尔德为角色提供"一个……成长空间"的技巧颇为赞赏，因为通过描述人物对社会环境的反应，作家可以更好地塑造人物（200）。从这个意义上讲，《家庭女教师》中的人物塑造是不完整的，因为作家只给予了女主人公有限的行动自由。此外，由于女主人公的意识是作家选用的唯一具有解释权的视角，幻想世界有时会因为缺乏和环境的对应而失去了与现实世界的关联。

然而，《家庭女教师》只是曼斯菲尔德早期人物塑造的实验成果之一，因为在此之前的作品，包括那些收集在《在德国公寓里》里的小说，其人物塑造充其量只能算是素描性质。在其早期作品中，主人公彼此之间以及他们与整个社会环境之间的联系，通常只能通过薄弱的故事情节里直接涉及的那些事件才得以建立。有时她的人物就像《一件稚气但十分自然的事》中那个爱幻想的女主人公一样，干脆在完全与世隔绝的生活环境中流连忘返。

在后来的作品中，曼斯菲尔德能够在更为复杂的人物关系网中，对幻想和现实之间的互动关系作出更为充分的揭示，并通过这个途径来探索那个"内在的人"。例如在《幸福》中，尽管伯莎的意识仍然主宰着叙事声音，但人物塑造主要还是依赖于她对一群复杂的人作出想象中的观察和反应，其中包括她的丈夫哈利、一个神秘而难以捉摸的女人珀尔以及他们那些举止怪诞的波希米亚朋友们。在《我不会讲法语》（"Je Ne Parle Pas Français"）这篇小说中，毛丝这个人物的塑造基本上是通过两个男人对她的不同反应来实现的。两个版本的毛丝在不断地纠正着彼此，而两个男主人公——迪克和"我"，则不停地在幻想世界里进进出出，因而读者对人物和情境的判断在不停地经受着调整和操控。在《一个无趣的男人》（"The Man Without a Temperament"）中，曼斯菲尔德则采用了一种新的人物塑造技巧。她将旅馆选为叙事背景，这样不仅能建立起一种更为广阔的社会视野，而且还允许人们从多重角度来观察和描述那个陷入悲哀生活困境的主人公。然而，无论在人际关系的复杂性上还是在人物塑造的深度上，都没有一篇小说超越了曼斯菲尔德的半自传体作品《序曲》——那是她整体创作中篇幅最长同时也最受瞩目的一篇小说。

在《序曲》里，曼斯菲尔德从她熟悉的主题中编织出生活真相，这个主题即"人物的个人化或理想化的看法"与"他/她对物质世界的感知"之间的冲突，或者"个人愿景……受到来自家庭角色所要求的传统职责的威胁"（Peterson 387）。在这个故事中，作者再次采用了通过揭示分裂的自我和随之而来的白日梦现象来塑造人物的写作技巧，但这一次人物被放置在了更宽广的社会背景之下。不同于《家庭女教师》，其女主角（即家庭教师）所经历的危机是通过一个戏剧性的事件——一次德国之旅以及与一位陌生人的相遇——来铺陈的，《序曲》中的人物是在参与和应对普通家庭生活的过程中获得了省察自我的能力。他们在幻想和现实中所扮演的每个角色，不仅构成了他们作为个体存在时对生活的看法，同时也暴露了他们作为社会存在时对彼此的态度。由于他们既梦想拥有别样生活，同时又能接受生活的现状，所以他们不会陷入个体人格彻底碎裂的境地。

《序曲》的故事以琳达·伯纳尔为核心人物编织了一张家庭网络。她是妻子，同时也是母亲、女儿和姐姐，但她发现很难协调这些角色，因为它们各自的功能是相互矛盾的。她对母亲费尔菲尔德太太在实际事务和精神情绪上的双重依赖，使她自己成了一个无能的母亲，而她对生育的厌恶则危及她与丈夫斯坦利的婚姻。另一方面，她作为妻子的角色使她与漂亮且单身的妹妹贝莉尔之间的关系变得有些微妙。然而，曼斯菲尔德在这个故事中主要的关注点并不在于这些公开职责之间的冲突，而是在于这些角色与琳达个人版本的理想化自我之间的差异。对理想化自我的追求，即灵魂的苦役，也构成了她这个人物形象的塑造过程。

琳达分裂的自我最初体现在她公开的和私下的母亲角色的划分上。当她展现自己公开的母亲身份时，尽管没有什么真实的感情，她还是为三个女儿提供了相对舒适富裕的生活。当她进入私下的母亲角色时，她把孩子看作是可耻的"性游击战"中的意外战利品，是强加于她的不相干事件（Fullbrook 85）。带有讽刺意味的是：主要生活在现实中的公开的母亲角色是遥不可及、模糊难辨、捉摸不定的，而总是漫游在幻想世界里的那个私下版本的母亲，则是有形的、具体的。前者努力支撑着沉重的面具，后者则渴望摆脱面具。

在小说的开场，琳达对孩子们的漠不关心就已经显而易见，当时伯纳尔一家正计划搬家。富布鲁克在其评著中深刻地洞察了小说以搬家为开场的重要隐喻意义：

> 搬家本身就是一种隐喻，指的是角色因暂时与习惯和常规角色脱节所产生的改变的可能性……这无疑意味着一个疏远和脱离从前的自我角色和生活环境的机会，从而促使角色的一系列自我意识活跃起来。（67—68）

环境变迁势必带来新的心境，正是怀着对这种新心境的热切期盼，琳达将自己置身于这场忙碌混乱的迁移行动之中。她告别旧身份的表现之一，就是决定把女儿凯赛娅和洛蒂留在塞缪尔·约瑟夫斯家里，她宣称这两个女儿并不在她的"绝对必需品"之列（*Bliss and Other Stories* 1）。

当两个女儿经过一夜的疲惫旅程终于随后抵达新家时，琳达甚至"连眼皮都没睁开瞧一瞧"（12）。她努力想告别过去，但结果却是所有的旧日"头痛之事"卷土重来。她在新房子里度过的第一个夜晚就做了个奇怪的梦。她梦到她和父亲在围场上散步，发现了脚边有一只"毛茸茸的小球"般的鸟。在她温柔的抚摸下，那鸟开始膨胀起来，最后变成了一个"长着个光光的大脑袋的婴儿，有一张咧开的鸟嘴，一开一合着"。她惊恐万状地醒来，只见斯坦利"站在窗口，在拉起威尼斯款百叶窗帘"（20）。这个梦反映了她醒来时的恐惧——她可以接受婴儿的存在，只要它像梦中那只毛茸茸的小鸟一样和她保持着一段安全距离，但是一个日益长大的孩子却威胁到她的自由，这对她来说是场彻头彻尾的噩梦。在梦中她一看到膨胀的婴儿就畏缩，这个梦境和她现实生活中两个母亲角色的碰撞和冲突产生了对应关系。

琳达对于母亲身份的矛盾情绪反映在了她对孩子们的态度，尤其是对凯赛娅的态度上。凯赛娅是她三个女儿中最懂事、最敏感的一位。琳达在花园里与凯赛娅偶遇的那个场景是非常具有启示意义的，这次相遇是这对母女之间唯一一次真正的心灵碰触。当凯赛娅提出关于芦荟树的问题时，琳达猝不及防，还没来得及戴上冷漠的面具：

> "妈妈，这是什么？"凯赛娅问。
>
> 琳达抬起头来看着那棵粗大肿胀，长着蛮叶硕干的植物。那树高高在上，好像在空中静止不动，然而它却紧紧抓着它所栖身的大地，它身下长的完全可以是爪子而不是根须。弯弯曲曲的叶子似乎在隐匿着什么秘密；鲁莽的树干直直地伸向空中，似乎没有风能撼动它。
>
> "那是一棵芦荟树，凯赛娅。"她母亲说。
>
> "它会开花吗？"
>
> "会的，凯赛娅，"琳达俯身对她微微一笑，半眯着眼睛说："一百年才开那么一次。"（34）

这是凯赛娅在向母亲请求心智上的引领，此时琳达再也不能回避女儿的需求了。尽管琳达的回答简短而乏味，但她那意味深长的微笑却替她说出了没有说出的话——这个微笑里蕴含着对芦荟树既赞赏又反感的杂陈情绪。琳达赞赏的是芦荟身上象征着女性力量和防御能力的特质，同时，树身的"肿胀"却又让她厌恶，因为它令人联想到性攻击的姿态。更值得探究的是琳达对这棵树开花能力的复杂感受。它那高贵而罕见的开花时刻提醒她人类衍繁能力的崇高意义，却也同时让她想起她生命中已经承受过的、还将继续承受下去的生育创痛。两个分裂的母亲角色在对芦荟树的沉思中第一次找到了统一点，她的幻想世界与现实世界也第一次有了重叠。对这棵怪异树木的共同兴趣，使得原本疏远的母女之间显露出愿意彼此沟通的迹象。虽然凯赛娅还太小，无法理解母亲的复杂情绪，但她作为孩子和作为女性，一定是凭直觉意识到了这是一个心灵真正相通的重要时刻。通过呈现琳达身上既具备女性力量也带有女性弱点的两个侧面，曼斯菲尔德创造了一个立体的人物形象，这个形象的任何行为和反应都不是基于理念，而是基于她所经历的复杂困境。

琳达对斯坦利爱恨交织的感情，也是曼斯菲尔德用来探索这个复杂人物身上的多重自我身份的一个渠道。琳达被赋予了中产阶级妻子的角色，这个身份和她私底下的女人角色处在不停的对峙和冲突之中。前一个角色在很大程度上是透过丈夫的存在而得到折射的，而后一个角色则反映了她对社会面具的不安。曼斯菲尔德成功地将读者的关注点聚焦在琳达私底下的那个女人角色上。从表面上看，琳达也和斯坦利一样沉浸在中产阶级特有的自以为是姿态之中，接受了（尽管是无精打采地）他的富有阶层的价值体系。这个价值体系借用理查德·彼得森（Richard Peterson）的贴切短语来形容，即追求社会成功的"盖茨比情结"（389）。但是还有另一个被常规生活的压力扭曲到濒临灭绝的自我，仍在挣扎着试图摆脱传统婚姻的束缚。这就是我们第二天早上在新居里所看到的琳达。随着斯坦利离家上班，前门砰的一声撞上，琳达的妻子角色暂告终结，她立即进入了另一个自我。新居的新鲜感还没来得及消散，她就已经对新环境显露出厌烦：

所有家具都各居其所——全套的零碎家什——她这样称呼它们。甚至连照片都好好地摆在壁炉架上方，药瓶放在洗漱台上的架子上。她的衣服——她的户外用品、一件紫色的披肩和一顶带羽毛的圆帽——斜搭在一张椅子上。她看着它们，真希望自己能离开这座房子。她看见自己驾着一辆小马车离开这些物件，离开每一个人，甚至连手都不挥一挥。（20—21）

家里的整洁和秩序，只适宜于在她承当着斯坦利妻子的角色的时候，而此刻却让她感觉恼怒和窒息。当她公开的妻子角色随着丈夫的离去而消失时，私下的那个自我就积极地参与到对生活其他可能性的幻想之中。她害怕如果她"自暴自弃、不抱怨……沉默、一动不动"，"它们"（即那些追着她的神秘邪恶力量）就会将她生吞活剥，不留下任何痕迹（25）。

一待斯坦利下班回来，焦躁不安、沉湎于幻想的琳达迅速退回到面具之后。她不温不火地回吻了他，但很快就把他的注意力转移到孩子们身上。她忍受着他面对食物的饕餮胃口，为了避开他的进一步身体亲近，她走开去到院子里赏月。在她的幻想中，月亮遥远的清辉即使不能给她指出一条逃路，至少也能让她看见超越日常琐碎的可能性。可是矛盾的是，现实中月亮的清辉却使她忍不住颤抖起来。她觉得冷，于是决定"离开窗户，坐到斯坦利旁边的脚凳上"（40），这个男人让她既渴望又讨厌。如果说观赏芦荟树的那个场景展示了琳达和凯赛娅之间唯一的一个心灵交流时刻，那么这个赏月场景就意味着琳达私下的那个自我向斯坦利的妻子角色缴械投降，幻想终究不敌现实。就这样，当这两个角色交替地支配着琳达的情绪时，她的生活就被划分为两个部分：长时间的缄默，夹杂着几个灵光闪现的叛逆时刻。

幻想场景将生活的分裂性公开化，给了我们机会从客观和主观两方面来观察评判琳达的性格，客观是当她在扮演妻子角色的时候，而主观是在我们被带入她的私密想法中时。这种分裂性之所以没有演化至失控状态，还得归功于琳达对生活现状的被动接受。尽管人们所期待的中产阶级妻子的行为模式抑制了那个不停地蠢蠢欲动的隐藏着的自我，但她在幻想中寻找解脱和慰藉的能力使得现实不至于变得无法承受。正是人生的这种分裂性和由此导致的荒谬，令她在夜游之时"默默发笑"：

> "我这么珍惜自己的身子图什么呢？我还会不断地生孩子，斯坦利还会不断地赚钱，孩子们和花园都会越来越大，园子里会有整队整队的芦荟树供我挑选。"（62—63）

生活的分裂性也体现在伯纳尔家庭成员的分裂上。按照性别和性情，这个家庭可以分为既同时存在而又相互排斥的两个阵营。斯坦利是伯纳尔家庭的一家之主，他的形象特征表现在他完全依赖外部价值来解释现实世界。对他而言，除了物质所包含的内容之外别无其他真理。与其恰恰相反，《序曲》中的女性世界则排斥正统男性版本的真相，她们用更为主观、可能超越物质王国范畴的方式来重新定义现实。

伯纳尔家族的大多数女性都被赋予了做白日梦的能力，这个能力与她们惯常的角色扮演有着自然的关联。她们的意识所吸纳的现实世界信息，是经过了白日梦的过滤的，这个筛选过程就揭示了她们的一些个性特质。例如，琳达把芦荟树想象成"一艘船""远远地划过花园的树梢"（60），表明了她尽管受预期的社会角色的束缚，但她仍然拥有一个女人的叛逆本性。同样地，爱丽丝不断演习"最奇妙的对应话语……来回答那些她知道永远不会问到她的问题"（54），则暴露了她恭顺和虚荣的个性。她依据各人在家庭中的不同地位而采取不同的态度来对待每个伯纳尔家庭成员，这是她保全自己的方法。

贝莉尔·费尔菲尔德的梦想也表明了她的性格。例如，她在镜子面前的自恋幻想时刻，传达出她对生活的终极虚假的恐惧已经浮到了意识表层。在她看来，镜中的映象似乎没那么虚假，只是更难以捉摸而已，而制造出那个镜像的原版自我，才是她最为厌恶的：

> 镜子里的那个玩意儿跟她有什么关系？她为什么一直盯着看？她瘫

坐在床边，把头埋在胳膊里。

"哎，"她哭喊着："我真是可悲——真是太可悲了。我知道自己愚蠢、刻薄、虚荣；我总是在扮演角色。我一刻也没做真正的自己。"（68）

这种虚假感也体现在贝莉尔在伯纳尔家庭中扮演的不同角色上。当她和斯坦利在一起时，她幻想用机灵巧妙的风情来篡夺琳达的妻子角色。而面对凯赛娅和爱丽丝时，她则把自己想象成是良师和主妇，来报复自己寄于姐姐篱下而蒙受的耻辱。而面对琳达时，她则是一个争夺母爱的妹妹。这些角色和伴随而来的幻想结合在一起，从不同的角度建立了她的终极人格——她是个不安分、任性的女人，她在生活中的不快乐很大程度上是因为她找不到"真实"的自我。

贝莉尔的幻想也反映了曼斯菲尔德作品中许多未婚女主人公的共同恐惧——她们害怕由于找不到丈夫而遭受社会的排斥。就像《我不会讲法语》中的毛丝和《声乐课》（"The Singing Lesson"）中那个神经质的音乐老师一样，贝莉尔也指望着用婚姻提供的保障来拯救自己。她选择年轻的意中人作为幻想世界的中心，以此来减轻多重自我相互抗衡的痛苦，这就形成了她和琳达之间的相互对照。贝莉尔的角色是通过激情的直接表述来界定的，而若想进入琳达的世界，却只有通过基于直觉的理解。

汉金提醒我们注意《序曲》中白日梦的不同动机：

> 幻想或白日梦是凯赛娅、琳达、贝莉尔和多迪共有的习惯，但这四个年轻人物的性格又有着很大的不同。对凯赛娅和琳达而言，幻想是一种几乎不自觉的活动，是压抑的焦虑受某一外在事物或事件的驱使，浮到了她们内心的表层。但对贝莉尔和多迪来说，这却是一种有意识的放纵，幻想或白日梦让她们从生活常规中解脱出来，使她们至少在想象中满足未能实现的愿望。（*Confessional Stories* 126）

汉金的观察是精确的，但不够完整。对上述所有人物而言，幻想不仅仅是一种逃脱或是一种用想象的经历来替代日常单一生活的冲动。由于它对生活不间断的、习惯性的侵扰，幻想也成了生活本身不可分割的一个部分。于是，对幻想的描述也就顺理成章地成了人物塑造的一个部分。当幻想进入现实生活时，人物的生存能力就会随着这个新增添的维度而得到明显的拓展。由于存在与想象之间的界限是纤细的，人物的主观世界因而变得越加复杂，人物的塑造也随之变得越加具有挑战性。

在《小说面面观》（Aspects of the Novel）一书中，E. M. 福斯特（E. M. Forster）把小说人物区分为"扁平的"和"圆润的"两种。他认为"扁平的人物形象是构建于一个单一的想法或特质之上的"；而圆润的人物形象则随时能显示出"延展的生命"的特征（83）。伯纳尔一家人是可信的，因为他们拥有这种可以获得延展的生活经验的丰富潜力。例如，读者会在凯赛娅身上发现生活的无限可能性。曼斯菲尔德通过对凯赛娅幻想世界的探索发掘了这些可能性，而这个幻想世界把作为孩子的凯赛娅和分裂的成人世界联系在一起。虽然小说是从多重视角叙述的，但许多故事场景实际上是经过了凯赛娅意识的过滤。由于过滤的过程是主观的、带有选择性的，凯赛娅选定的视角反映了她潜在的性格发展。萨拉琳·戴利（Saralyn Daly）在仔细观察了凯赛娅在《序曲》中两天的行为举止之后，得出了一个令人信服的结论：凯赛娅与她的外祖母费尔菲尔德太太有着相通之处，因为二者都热爱秩序（70—71）。

在薛立丹家里，除了斯坦利之外，另一位缺乏对事务作出情绪性反应能力的人是费尔菲尔德太太。她所看重的想法，大多与功利主义价值观相关。例如，当琳达在沉思芦荟树所象征的自由和贞洁的可能性时，费尔菲尔德太太则在期待果酱丰产的好季节到来。在一些最能说明问题的情节中，凯赛娅表现出了某些显而易见与费尔菲尔德太太相似的特质。但具有讽刺意味的是，凯赛娅模仿外祖母的实用主义特质，却是通过幻想的媒介来实现的。当她被母亲留在塞缪尔·约瑟夫斯家里时，她就像费尔菲尔德太太在类似境况下通常会做的那样，在那座废弃的老房子里寻找任何有实用价值的东西。她发现了一个"外表漆黑闪亮、内里是红色的药盒子，里头装着一团棉花"（6）。但关于这个盒子的实用功能，她却只能想出一个奇幻的用途——"储放鸟蛋"(6)。她以同样的方式，用一个"异想天开的把戏"来实现一个火柴盒的"实际"用途，即把紫罗兰装在其中当作送给外祖母的惊喜礼物。还有一次，在一场孩子们幻想出来的"扮演淑女"的游戏中，凯赛娅极其精确地呈现了费尔菲尔德太太对秩序的热爱：

> 精美的晚餐正在水泥台阶上烘烤着。她（凯塞娅）把桌布摊在一张粉红色的花园座椅上。她在每个人面前放了两个用天竺葵叶设想成的盘子、一把松针叉子和一把树枝刀。一片月桂叶上摆着三个雏菊头，那是她设想的水煮蛋；几个灯笼花的花瓣是冷牛肉片；还有几个由泥土、水和蒲公英种子做成的可爱的小甜饼，她决定用帕瓦蛋壳端上她在里头煮好的巧克力酱。(43)

此处虚构的厨房与外祖母的世界遥相呼应，秩序在那里占据上风，"一切都是成双成对的"(29)。

家里斩鸭头的场景进一步说明：在面对混乱时，凯赛娅和费尔菲尔德太太有着如出一辙的恐惧。当帕特开始演示"爱尔兰国王是如何剁下鸭头"时(48)，喷出的血不仅使凯赛娅领悟了死亡这个独属于成人世界的奥秘，而且也使她意识到了既定生活模式里所存在着的威胁。她狂喊着"把头放回去！把头放回去"(51)，这既表达了她对生命的丧失所感受到的哀伤，也显示了她企图"恢复原有秩序"的幻想——正如戴利所述(71)那样。

读者也会在凯赛娅的幻想世界中找到了琳达的影子。琳达厌恶来自男人的动物般的性威胁，这种威胁以塞缪尔·约瑟夫斯家那几个霸道男孩的形式，延续出现在凯赛娅的意识之中。尽管对斯坦利充满了仇恨，琳达却无可奈何地选择接受了生活的残酷安排；而凯赛娅在面对约瑟夫家男孩们所造成的伤害时（无论是真实的还是在幻想中被夸大了的），她也都假装毫不在意：

> 哼！她根本不在乎！一滴泪珠顺着她的脸颊流下来，但她并没在哭。她不可能在那些可恶的塞缪尔·约瑟夫斯们面前哭泣。她低头坐着，

眼泪慢慢滴了下来。她用舌头轻轻一舔就把它接住了，趁谁也还没看见之际，就把它吃了下去。（5）

　　和琳达一样，凯赛娅的幻想经历也与她清醒时的想法相互呼应。例如，她对来自男人的性威胁的认识，经常会以动物突然向她奔跑并膨胀的形式出现在她的噩梦里。在去往新居的路上，凯赛娅告诉店员说："我讨厌奔跑的动物。我常常梦见动物朝我奔跑过来——甚至是骆驼——它们奔跑的时候，头都肿胀得天一样大"（10）。琳达称斯坦利为"我的纽芬兰犬"，在她对斯坦利的描述中，我们也看到了类似的恐怖："要是他不这样冲她跳，不那么大声地吠叫，不那样饥渴地充满爱欲地望着她就好了；对她来说他太强壮了；她从小就一直讨厌那些冲她奔来的东西"（61）。就这样，通过这些幻想媒介，曼斯菲尔德建立了凯赛娅与费尔菲尔德太太和琳达之间的关联，进而探索了凯赛娅个性充分发展的两种可能性，这些可能性反映并囊括了她外祖母的务实和她母亲的敏感。

　　在谈到人物塑造时，M. H. 阿布拉姆斯（M. H. Abrams）对"讲述"（telling）和"展示"（showing）这两种塑造方法作了广义上的区分（21）。现在人们普遍认为：把关注点从情节转向意识、从告知转向启示，也就是从"讲述"转向"展示"，在很大程度上是曼斯菲尔德在人物塑造上的创新之举。当我们把幻想元素作为曼斯菲尔德塑造人物的成功原因之一来研究时，我们不应忽略内心独白在强化"展示"过程中的作用。通过描述人物对幻想的沉湎以及传达这种沉湎的方式，曼斯菲尔德深入探讨了她的主人公的多个分裂自我和由此产生的多重存在。由于不必依赖叙述者作为唯一的信息来源，读者的视角得到了很大拓展。曼斯菲尔德交替使用着作家的声音和人物的内心独白，因而可以从远距离和近距离两种角度来审视她的人物。她在人物的幻想世界里自由进出，由此将他们的内心想法和外部世界连接起来。当读者有机会比较这两者的不同之处时，人物塑造就达到了相对客观的效果。

　　在《家庭女教师》中，我们可以找到巧妙地运用内心独白的范例。通过那些记录女教师在火车上的长篇遐想的段落，曼斯菲尔德达到了一箭双雕的目的：既展示了女主人公对生活的幻想是她在慕尼黑遭遇悲剧的内在原因，也揭示了外在客观世界存在的邪恶力量，尽管这个客观世界是被女主人的主观意识所扭曲了的。与此同理，贝莉尔·费尔菲尔德在镜前的自恋冥想，也达到了连接两个世界的目的——一个是充满了可能性的主观世界，另一个是一成不变的客观世界。

在曼斯菲尔德的其他小说中，我们也发现了内心独白的这种功能。例如，在小说《旅途》（"The Voyage"）中，作者对旅行场景的描述经常被主人公费内拉的静默观察所打断，从而展现了这个小女主人公在透明的童年和无法预测的成人现实世界之间飘忽不定的存在。在小说《已故上校的女儿》（"The Daughters of the Late Colonel"）的结尾，读者发现康斯坦西娅站在已故父亲房间里那尊她最喜欢的佛像前，大声思考着："这是什么意思？她一直想要的到底是什么？这一切到底会导致什么？现在就告诉我？就现在"（*The Garden Party and Other Stories* 127）。她的浮想联翩暴露了她焦急而徒劳地想在实现个人梦想和尽孝道的现实之间找到调和之处的愿望。在这些显示内在关联的时刻中，人物形象无论在小说主题还是哲学角度上都变得真实起来，因为它们传达了"二元对立（即生命的丰富潜力与人类经历中不可避免的残酷性之间，存在着不可调和的分裂，这种分裂必定导致绝望）"的"整体模式"（Berkman 159）。

第三章

幻想：意象和象征

　　许多评论家都已注意到凯瑟琳·曼斯菲尔德与法国象征主义之间的相似性，尤其是她在艺术实践中一直坚持的象征主义理论。克莱尔·汉森和安德烈·格尔认为这一理论的本质是"仅通过具体意象来传达抽象的思想或情感状态，具体意象在其间所起的作用是给抽象思想或情感状态提供'客观关联'"（50）。早在1908年，曼斯菲尔德就在亚瑟·西蒙斯（Arthur Symons）所著的《散文与诗歌研究》（*Studies in Prose and Verse*）一书的注释中表明：她拒绝使用分析性的描述，而偏爱通过具有暗示性的"人物特定行为"来揭示真相：

　　　　坚持分析描述法的人会非常详细地描述灵魂的状态，描述每个行为的隐秘动机，似乎动机比行为本身还要重要得多。支持客观叙述法的人则会提供事件演变的结果，而不卷入对潜在过程的描述。他们通过最细微的姿势来唤出灵魂的状态，即把肉包裹着的骨头呈现出来——这于我而言就是艺术家的方式，艺术在我看来是**纯粹的愿景**——事实上，我就是个信奉客观描述的人。（*The Critical Writings of Katherine Mansfield* 140）

　　曼斯菲尔德的文学创作见证了她对"这种排他与暗示的艺术"所作的不懈努力（Hanson and Gurr 50）。通过考察她的写作生涯，我们发现：当她作品中的动机分析完全让位于一系列精心安排的意象时，她就抵达了艺术创作的巅峰。这些意象具有双重意义：从象征意义上说，它们代表了小说人物未能实现的梦想或幻想；从主题角度上说，这些意象构成了它们赖以存在的现实环境的一个部分。就总体而言，当意象模式既满足象征又满足主题的需要时，叙事便是成功的。在意象与主题功能脱节的小说中，意象所起的象征作用通常是不自然的、强加的。芦荟树之所以会成为《序曲》中有效的中心意象，完全是因为它实现了这种双重功能。它不仅表明了琳达内心想摆脱性束缚的渴望，而且还有益于塑造伯纳尔新居的环境，而这个环境是人物情绪变化的重要因素。同样，《园会》（"The Garden Party"）中作为意象使用的那顶优雅的黑帽子，既能根据主题的需要营造园会的气氛，又象征了富裕阶层女性的虚荣心，而虚荣正是薛立丹家庭成员的幻想世界的重要构成部分。

然而，并不是曼斯菲尔德的每篇作品都在这方面取得了同等的成功的。《鸽子先生和鸽子太太》（"Mr. and Mrs. Dove"）显而易见就是一个失败的例子。在这篇小说中，曼斯菲尔德企图在鸽子为了求偶而低头鞠躬和年轻男主人公雷吉纳德对真爱的执着追求之间找到某种相似，但是由于与基本叙事主题缺乏内在联系，这种（表面）相似以及随之而来的象征意义就被大大削弱了。《苍蝇》（"The Fly"）是另外一个失败的例子。由于无法与主题语境紧密契合，小说中的主要意象苍蝇的象征意义就大大地打了折扣。昆虫的命运和人类命运之间的类比关系"简单得近乎粗糙"（Hanson and Gurr 130），所以读者在她其他作品里发现的丰富暗示意义，在这里几乎消失殆尽。

对曼斯菲尔德来说，艺术的成熟过程也是意象模式走向多样化和复杂化的过程。这个过程是痛苦不堪，异常曲折的。约翰·米德尔顿·莫里试图将之总结为四个分明的阶段，每一个阶段都带有曼斯菲尔德自身情感经历的印记：

（1）对生活强烈的厌恶——《**序曲**》之前的作品特点；

（2）快乐地、充满爱意地接受生活——这个状态在《**序曲**》中首次得到了完整的表述；

（3）而后是对生活强烈的幻灭感和厌恶感——**"没有比这更大的痛苦了"**（此句原文为意大利语——引者注）——这在《**幸福**》中首次进行了完整表达。随着阅历加深，幻灭感和厌恶感渐渐沉淀为非常深沉的绝望，这在《**我不会讲法语**》中可以找到端倪。最后就到了第四阶段；

（4）连这种绝望她也容忍接纳了。她最后阶段的作品正是由于接受了绝望而趋于完美。（*Katherine Mansfield and Other Literary Studies* 88）

遗憾的是，后来的评论家都过于被莫里的判断所左右，倾向于严格按照时间顺序来划分曼斯菲尔德的艺术成就，而不是将其视为一个连贯的整体。通过考察我们可以发现：其实曼斯菲尔德的创作并不能完全按照莫里的顺序来划分。例如，莫里认为《序曲》是曼斯菲尔德在"快乐地、充满爱意地接受生活"的情况下创作的，但小说中的琳达和贝莉尔试图逃避日常生活的束缚却徒劳无果，她们身上明显带着近乎绝望的哀伤，她们和曼斯菲尔德后期的女主人公一样充满悲剧和无助感。另一方面，从她去世前几个月写下的《苍蝇》和《帕克大妈的一生》（"The Life of Ma Parker"）中，我们可以清晰地听见她对人类悲惨境遇的毫不掩饰的强烈抗议。生活的悲楚并没有像莫里所述那样把她的主人公们驯服成完全听天由命的人。尽管如此，莫里把《序曲》当作是曼斯菲尔德艺术生涯的分水岭是合理而具有洞察力的。

在曼斯菲尔德《序曲》之前的作品（包括她的少年习作）中，构成她笔下人物的幻想世界的那些意象都是相对单一而缺乏变化的。这些意象常常是以一个人的形象来体现生活中未能实现的欲望，比如一位慈爱的父亲或母亲，或是一位情人和灵魂伴侣。这个梦中人要么纯粹是凭幻想创造的，就像《一个理想的家庭》中温柔的白雪公主式的女人，和《我的盆栽》中那个神秘而捉摸不定的林中女子；要么是通过想象将真实人物转化为一个半神式的人物，就像《朱丽叶》（"Juliet"）中才华横溢的音乐家大卫和《女家庭教师》中的"神仙祖父"。

在曼斯菲尔德的早期实验性作品中，主人公们只存活于与世隔绝的幻想世界中，活动范围相当受限。而且他们的幻想世界几乎是完全围绕着他们与梦中人或是真实或是想象的联系而展开的。非常具有典型意义的一篇小说就是《一件稚气但十分自然的事》，它创作于1913年，但却是在作者去世后的1924年才发表的。切丽·汉金将它描述为"年轻的梦想与成人现实的第一次相遇"（*Confessional Stories* 97）。

《一件稚气但十分自然的事》是以亨利和艾德娜这两个年轻人在开往伦敦的通勤列车上的邂逅而开场的。曼斯菲尔德使用意象表述了亨利对白日梦的沉迷，直击读者心灵。亨利为一首题为《一件稚气但十分自然的事》的小诗所迷，因为"这上面有梦的微笑"（130），他差点为此错过火车，但这让他意外地遇见了艾德娜。亨利被描述成一个因"一切无聊至极的事情（139）"而早早地感到生活乏味无趣的年轻人，他把生活的乏味归咎于来自社会的压迫感。他声称"是人让事情变成这样的——愚蠢啊，只要你能避开他们，你就会安全而开心"（140）。他很快在艾德娜身上找到了惺惺相惜的感觉，因为她梦幻般的存在让他觉得自己可以远离人山人海的社会环境。

曼斯菲尔德用来描绘埃德娜的意象是奇异而神秘的，关于她的一切似乎都像披着一层纱。她的脸和肩膀因其瀑布般的长发遮挡只隐约可见；她的手因戴着手套而无法看见；甚至她的声音也是模糊而悠远的。当她抬起脸庞时，亨利终于可一窥其容颜，但她灰色的眼睛却始终"隐藏在帽檐的阴影之下"，嘴唇也只是"微微张开着"（132）。这个半是人半是精灵的女子很快就整个占据了亨利的幻想世界。她那梦幻般的存在使亨利的心膨胀得"越来越大，像个巨大的神奇的泡泡在颤动着——他害怕打碎这一切，甚至都不敢呼吸"（133）。由于他对她的沉迷，他与鲜活的现实生活的联系就变得微乎其微了：

> 他试图记起遇见艾德娜之前的生活，但他无法回到那些日子里去了。它们被艾德娜遮挡住了。头发如金盏花、带着怪异的梦幻般笑容的艾德娜将亨利从头到脚整个地填满了。她成了他的呼吸，他的食物，他的饮料。他行走时随身带着艾德娜那闪亮的光环，那光将他与现实世界隔离开来，用自身的美照亮了所及的一切。（151）

随着主题的深化，曼斯菲尔德采用的意象持续地指向艾德娜的神秘特质。他们第二次会面时，读者发现艾德娜是突然出现在亨利前的，仿佛来自仙境，"白雾缭绕……消散又重新聚起，形成飘摇不定的花环"（135）。当亨利谈论着他们设想中未来的乌托邦新家时，她听着，脸上"浮起梦幻般的笑容"（147）。最能表明她虚幻特质的是她躲闪着不与爱人产生任何身体接触。亨利对此半是沉迷半是害怕，他需要身体的亲密接触来消除彼此间的距离。"他想亲吻艾德娜，将她搂住，紧紧地抱着她，用吻感受她脸上的温热，吻到他窒息为止，就这样把梦憋醒。"（152）他的矛盾心理构建出了这篇小说的主要讽刺意义：一个在很大程度上依靠幻想生存的人，竟然会在他自己的梦幻世界中缺乏安全感。

　　在包括《一个理想的家庭》和《朱丽叶》在内的少年习作中，曼斯菲尔德经常召唤死神来弥合幻想与现实之间的鸿沟，这样她笔下的人物便可以和梦中人永远生活在一起。但在《一件稚气但十分自然的事》里，与濒死状态相似的梦境却很嘲讽地让主人公更加贴近了现实。亨利醒来时，艾德娜满足了他对理想人际关系的幻想，她最终同意和他产生亲密的肢体接触，甚至愿意和他一起"过家家"——那是一个幻想中的乌托邦爱情王国。而在他的梦境中，她却背叛了他的信任，改变了自己的形状，先是变成了一只白色的飞蛾，之后又变成了一个手里捏着一份电报的阴险狡诈的小女孩。正如汉金所指出的那样："幻想的要求"与"现实的需要"之间不可调和的关系，决定了小说必然会以那样的方式结尾：

　　　　他（亨利）和艾德娜走到一起完全是因为他们相信自己是与常人不
　　同的人。由于他们的虚幻存在是建立在这一前提之上的，任何接受自己
　　是正常人的举动，即使不一定破坏，但也势必会威胁到他们之间的关系
　　（ *Confessional Stories* 88 ）。

　　与曼斯菲尔德其他早期象征主义实验作品一样，这篇小说显然是不成熟的。尽管她偏爱通过具体的暗示性意象来揭示灵魂状态，但这些叙事背后的象征意义却是通过遥远而抽象、几乎只具符号意义的人物形象来传达的。艾德娜占据了亨利的整个社会视野，因而阻碍了幻想世界与现实世界之间的互动联系，从而将故事背景转化成了半童话式的场景。

　　随着曼斯菲尔德逐渐成熟，这种用符号方式展现一个作为核心象征意

象的"梦幻人物"的写作方法渐渐消失了，自《序曲》之后的小说见证了意象模式的明显变化。为探索幻想和模拟现实间的相互关系，曼斯菲尔德不再在一个单一的概念化的梦幻人物身上寻找她的意象和隐喻，她的视野拓展到了广袤的大自然界。这一时期，她的信件和日志中都充溢着对大自然的温馨感情。"仿佛她所生活的机械化、军事化的世界在她的想象中基本不存在"（Zinman 458）。这里的"想象"一词完全可以用"幻想"来替代。这种在大自然中找到的丰富的意象，以其多元化和生命力指向了人类想象生活中的无限可能性，与此相比，现实是何等贫乏和一成不变。在《序曲》发表后很快就完成的《幸福》，是首批见证了曼斯菲尔德写作方法之变化的小说之一。

值得注意的是，《幸福》是曼斯菲尔德在第一次肺出血后几天之内完成的。由于当时她是独自一人被战火困在法国，在孤独中承受如此打击，更加倍了她对这种致命疾病的恐惧。但令人奇怪的是：这个打击反而激发了她对生活的炽烈之爱、对自然之美的热切欣赏之心。在肺疾急性发作的第二天，即1918年2月20日，她给莫里写了一封信，告诉他自己的这种心态：

> 我受这小小的打击之后便发生了一件怪事。我感觉我对外部世界的爱与渴望——我是说自然界——突然增加了千百万倍。当我想起草地上生长的小花，还有小溪，还有我们可以躺在上面观看云彩的地方——哦，我的心单纯地渴想这些情景——和你一起渴想它们（Letters to Murry 175）。

正如西尔维娅·伯克曼指出的，曼斯菲尔德的这种情绪"与《幸福》的根本主题——不为人类灾难所动的自然之美——是彼此相关的，而这种相关并非偶然"（107）。这个主题是作者通过围绕着小说人物（特别是伯莎·杨）所构造的一系列意象来实现的。

马文·马格拉纳在《凯瑟琳·曼斯菲尔德在〈幸福〉中的"自我"痕迹》（"Traces of Her 'Self' in Katherine Mansfield's 'Bliss'"）一文中，将伯莎"从幸福走向深度绝望"的"情感曲线图"归咎于她在一个下午和晚上的短暂时间里所经历的一系列发现。马格拉纳认为伯莎的发现之一是她丈夫与珀尔·富尔顿之间"突发的不忠"。读者也因此得知了一些先前未知的信息：

> 伯莎无法恢复（与珀尔的）神秘关系了；伯莎和孩子们的关系不如孩子们和保姆之间的关系牢靠；伯莎虽然是那群古怪的波希米亚伪知识分子的女主人，但这个身份并没有给她参与交流的资格，他们也同样没资格与她交流。（414）

但马格拉纳忽略了一个最基本的发现，这个发现能够导致并解释其他所有的发现，即伯莎发现了假设与事实、想象与真相之间的差异。这一发现是主题结构的主线。曼斯菲尔德基本上是通过不断变化的、把主人公与她周遭环境联系起来的意象模式，把这条主线传达给她的读者的。

曼斯菲尔德利用伯莎与太阳的直接关联，把伯莎呈现在一个虚假的幻想世界里——小说叙事由此展开。伯莎第一次在小说中的亮相，是伴随着一阵近乎歇斯底里的情绪爆发的，她自认为那是一种"幸福"感：

> 当你三十岁，走在自己所住街道的拐角处，突然间被一种幸福感淹没——绝对的幸福！——仿佛你猝然吞下了一片灿烂的午后阳光，它在你的怀里燃烧，向每一个分子、每一个手指和脚趾送出一小束火花。这时你能做什么呢？（*Bliss and Other Stories* 116）

当幻想支配着伯莎的情绪时，她与太阳的亲近变得愈发明显。在日常生活中，她发现自己"太冷了"（133），她的身体就像"一把被关在盒子里的稀有之极的小提琴"（116）。当她沉浸在幻想中时，她便觉得心中满怀激情与欲望，由内而外地燃烧起来。因此，太阳的比喻是成立的。

正是这种强烈的欲望驱使她做出奇怪的举动：她把晚宴上的水果摆成"两个金字塔般……光亮浑圆的"胸脯形状（118）；她突然间有股冲动要"热烈地、热烈地"抱住客厅的坐垫（122）。事实证明，这两种行为（即幻想中的性满足暗示）实际上是徒劳无果的，因为它们并不能"扑灭她心头的火"，而是"适得其反"（122）。伯莎的激情是暧昧而又复杂的，既包含她对丈夫哈利·杨显而易见的性渴望，也包含对她新近"发现"并声称"爱上了"的珀尔·富尔顿小姐隐秘的渴望（121）。

通过对比珀尔身上所呈现的月亮意象，伯莎在幻想场景中与太阳的联系得到了进一步确立。朱迪斯·S.尼尔曼（Judith S. Neaman）提醒我们注意珀尔身上明显的"月亮特质"，以此反衬出伯莎太阳般的温暖（244），但她将故事的母题追溯到圣经源头的企图却显得有些牵强附会。珀尔是在一个月光皎洁的夜晚被带进读者的视野的，她"一身银装，淡金色的头发上绑着一根银色的发带"。当她坐在哈利的身边摆弄着橘子时，她纤细的手指苍白到"好像透着光"（129—130）。她像月亮一样不可捉摸，高不可攀。她很少"直接"看人，眼睑"沉重"，笑容"怪异"，似笑非笑（128）。更能暴露她身上隐秘特质的是她那模糊而又遥远的声音，她说话时不断地低语暗示，传达的信息是含糊不清而非明晰准确的，导致的结果是误解而非理解。然而，在一种过度情绪化状态的驱使下，伯莎纵容自己去混淆想象与事实、幻想与存在之间的界限。她坚持把珀尔模棱两可的话理解为她抛给她的交流"信号"，尽管她的自信不时也伴有怀疑和困惑：

> 她（伯莎）根本弄不明白——真是太神奇了——她怎么能那么准确、那么迅速地猜到富尔顿小姐的心思呢？她从来没有怀疑过自己的正确，但她又有什么依据呢？**她的依据比没有还少**（强调为引者所加）。（130）

除了像月亮般难以捉摸之外，珀尔身上还带有许多别的可以引起各种猜测和联想的特质，伯莎对此深感困惑。例如，珀尔也让人联想起那只拖着影子爬过草地的灰猫。凯特·富布鲁克把它解读成她"既绝对超然又完全阴暗"的性取向（101—102）。两极化的意象及其产生的联想共同确立了珀尔存在的二元性，也从而决定了伯莎的幻想世界必然崩塌。富布鲁克对曼斯菲尔德采用的这一技巧表示赞赏，将其总结为"符号的选择和放置都非常巧妙、发人深思，它们的意义是通过暗示，而非明显的强调而得出的"（101）。

曼斯菲尔德在《幸福》中对象征主义渐趋成熟的运用手法，也表现在她对两极意象的和谐处理上。例如伯莎和珀尔就被描述成两个极端：一位像太阳一样炽烈通透，另一位却像月亮一样冷静、遥远而神秘，但这分化的两极却因着她们对伯莎花园里的梨树的共同依恋得到了和谐统一。

梨树的象征意味已经引起了大量的评议和讨论。包括切斯特·艾辛杰（Chester Eisinger）在内的一些评论家强调了这棵树的男性生殖特性，并因此把树和伯莎及珀尔共同慕求的哈利联系起来（Item 48）。包括沃尔特·E. 安德森（Walter E. Anderson）在内的其他人，则认为梨树是"一个综合象征，树的高度暗指了伯莎的同性恋愿望，而它丰盛的花朵则代表她对性的渴求"（400）。安德森进一步指出，梨树的花朵指向"她女性的性身份"，而它的"高大自信"则象征着"她的性感受中连她自己都还没有意识到的'男性'部分"（400）。上述两种说法都需要一些修正，因为前者没能正确解释梨树的开花状态，这是女性特质的明证；而后者并未把珀尔囊括进象征的范畴，因为同性恋的隐喻与珀尔并没有明显的联系。随着主题的发展，我们需要建立一种与梨树更加自然且符合逻辑的联系。我们注意到，梨树第一次进入故事，是当伯莎站在客厅窗边眺望花园，浑身洋溢着"幸福"感的时候：

> 花园尽头，靠着墙边的地方，有一棵高大细长的梨树，上面开满了丰盛的花朵；它完美地站立着，似乎在宁静中直指碧玉色的天空。即使隔着这么远，伯莎也不禁觉得树上没有一个未开的骨朵，或一片凋零的花瓣。（122）

很显然，伯莎被这棵树的原始生命迷住了。树上所有的花朵都在绽放，既没浪费的青春也没衰败的暮年，这一切都暗指伯莎女性生命的丰盛年华。仿佛是害怕因拖延而失去对其转瞬即逝的本质的把握，伯莎急急忙忙地宣称"这棵可爱的梨树"是"她自身生命的象征"（123）。

从外表看，伯莎的生活就像是这盛开的梨树一般完美而丰硕——显赫的社会声望、富硕的家境、唾手可得的时尚、文化魅力以及友情，她应有尽有。同样与这棵多产而"宁静"的树木相似的，还有他们夫妻之间的爱。正如伯莎认为的那样，他们已经度过了感情炙烈的风暴期，进入了成熟而稳定的阶段。然而，在这幻想中的完美之下，隐藏着一些她想要闭眼不看的阴影，一如在这生气勃勃的梨花之下行走着的那只丑猫，一看见它，她就打了个"奇怪的寒战"（122）。以上意象的使用，使这棵树与伯莎对生活本质的幻想之间产生了更密切的联系。直接威胁到这幸福憧憬的，是那未遂之愿的阴影。面对"令人毛骨悚然的"的现实，她选择"转身离开窗户"，开始"走来走去地漫步"（123）。

随着主题的推进，梨树与幻想的联系延伸至珀尔。故事快结束时，珀尔建议去看看花园。这时，伯莎的内心因接收到这个交心的"迹象"而激动得颤抖起来：

> 两个女人并肩站着观赏那棵亭亭玉立、满身繁花的梨树。这树虽然看上去静止不动，可当她们定睛仰望的时候，它宛如蜡烛的火苗，在清澈的夜空中向上伸展，直指天空，颤动着，越长越高——几乎快触碰到那轮银色圆月的边缘了。（131）

此时，两个女人身上的两种极端特质，即太阳般的热情和月亮般的宁静，在梨树这一意象中找到了和谐和统一。这是个难得的心有灵犀的时刻，她们二人在共同幻想着生命的无限潜能时，一起经历了忘我的境界：

> 她们站在那里多久了？两个人在某种程度上仿佛都被那不属于尘世的光环所吸引，完完全全地理解了彼此。她们都是另一个世界的生物，深藏在她们内心的幸福感在胸中燃烧着，像银色梨花那样从她们的头发和手上掉落。她们不知道在这个世界里到底要干什么。（131）

梨树的神秘特质加剧了曼斯菲尔德想要创造的象征效果。它的遥不可及呼应了两位女性梦想的虚幻性——她们绽放的青春和活力以及对完美生命的幻想都属于"另一个世界"。曼斯菲尔德通过梨树与人的愿望之间的类比，揭示了人类命运的另一组矛盾——人类既无法抑制对人际关系中的真和爱的渴望，也不能逃脱未能遂愿时的绝望，这两者总是相互交织的。

　　遥不可及的意象与其难以捉摸的含义之间的对应关系，在小说的其他段落也能找到。太阳是与伯莎有着显而易见关联的意象，其本质是不可靠近的。当我们意识到这一点时，我们也就知道伯莎与丈夫的性满足以及与珀尔的精神结合的愿望是注定不可实现的。而珀尔月亮般的高不可攀特质，却因她和哈利之间的下作关系而削弱了。一些批评家，如尼尔曼（Neaman 246）和马格拉纳（"Traces of Her 'Self'" 415），已注意到曼斯菲尔德的男性人物（包括哈利在内）对食物的欲望与他们过度的性欲之间的联系。但很少有人看出《幸福》中反复出现的食物意象与围绕着伯莎和珀尔的那些高雅向上的意象之间的鲜明对照。例如，哈利的词汇中充斥着指向动物器官和人体消化功能的词语。他描述和评估价值时最常用的词语有"一个好胃""冻肝""纯属胀气"或者"肾病"（122）。特别是在那天的晚宴中，他关乎食物的谈话里又带上了一层关于性的暗示：

　　　　哈利正在享受晚餐。他喜欢谈论饮食，这是他的一部分——呃，确切地说，不是他的本性，当然也不是在装腔作势——是他的——说不清楚是什么——他引以为荣地"对龙虾的白色肉体"和"又绿又冷，像埃及舞女的眼皮似的开心果冰"有着"无耻的贪婪之情"。（129）

　　用与食物相关的词语来阐明观点的习惯，在与哈利有交往的人中，即他的波希米亚朋友们身上，都可以找到例子。诺曼·奈特夫人（又名菲斯）谈到为雅各布·纳桑一家装饰房间时，她的设计是基于"一种炸鱼的主题设想，椅子的靠背形状像煎锅，窗帘上绣满了可爱的炸土豆片"（132）。在晚宴上，哈利的另一位宾客艾迪·沃伦引用了题为《胃病》（129）和《套餐》的作品，开篇是"为什么总是要喝番茄汤"（135）？就像伯莎的太阳和珀尔的月亮各有所指一样，这群人与食物的密切关系也显露了他们性格的一个部分——贪婪、装模作样、缺乏基本的想象力。伯莎和珀尔被赐予天体的特性，使她们能够高翔于幻想的精神王国，而哈利和他的朋友们则放纵于俗世欢乐，注定是要作为"这个世界的动物"被束缚在地球上。

在曼斯菲尔德的后期作品（尤其是她生命的最后几年中完成的作品里）所呈现的象征主义与我们在《序曲》和《幸福》中所见的已经有了明显的区别。我们可以看出一种回归中心意象的倾向，单一的象征性暗示再次被用来描述小说人物的幻想世界。例如，在《苍蝇》中，为生存而挣扎的可怜的小昆虫构成了故事的中心象征，尽管它的功能引起了评论界的热议。苍蝇被塑造成主人公幻想世界的焦点，事实上，它也是主人公可以用来想象"生活的其他选择"——即与全能的神交换位置——的唯一一件工具。曼斯菲尔德把一个儿子的死亡与一只苍蝇的死亡相提并论，尽管过于刻意，但她旨在"邀请读者在老板玩弄苍蝇的生命和上帝或诸神玩弄人的生命之间建立起一个形而上学的等式，因为两者都是'为了取乐'而已"（Hanson and Gurr 130）。在《帕克大妈的一生》中，我们可以再次看到这种对单一象征意象的依赖。对死去的孙子莱尼的回忆，给了这个憔悴的老女佣唯一的机会，让她可以沉浸在自己的幻想世界里，在那里现实不再存在，也不再能伤害到她。

曼斯菲尔德最后阶段的代表性作品之一是《布偶之屋》（"The Doll's House"），它与《园会》及《帕克大妈的一生》都被保罗·德兰尼（Paul Delany）称为"穷人简史"（short and simple annals of the poor）（7），这是借用了格雷（Gray）的《挽歌》（Elegy）中的一句话。故事的中心，实际上也是故事象征意义的唯一载体，是一个布偶之屋，叙事高潮是围绕着这座玩具房子展开的。房子是海伊夫人送给伯纳尔家孩子们的礼物，它在两个层面上激发了作者的叙述兴趣。首先，对伯纳尔家的女孩来说，甚至包括敏感且富有同情心的凯赛娅在内，它是财富和阶级差别的象征。但同时，它又是所有来看这座房子的女孩们的童年幻想化身。

对伯纳尔家的大女儿伊莎贝拉来说，拥有这座布偶之屋具有"真实而又虚幻的"意义（Maxwell-Mahon 48）。玩具房子刚送到时，孩子们，尤其是伊莎贝拉，立刻就发现最抓人眼球之处是它的精致——它可以与她们自己的住宅相媲美。这所房子既是伊莎贝拉童年现实的一部分，也是她童年幻想的一部分。它能够让她同时扮演两个角色——一个是真实角色：作为家里的长女，她对这座房子有天然的优先权；一个是想象的"房子女主人"的角色，这个角色让她可以用富有阶层特有的傲慢，来占有和保护自己的财产：

> 学校铃声响起之前，她们（伯纳尔家的女孩）迫不及待地要告诉每一个人，要显示——哦，要显摆一下她们的布偶房。
>
> 伊莎贝拉说："我要告诉她们，因为我是最大的。你们两个过会儿再加进来说。但是我要第一个说。"
>
> 谁也没回嘴。伊莎贝拉霸道，但她总是对的。洛蒂和凯塞娅太知道当老大的权利了。她们擦着路边厚厚的毛茛行走，一言未发。
>
> "还有，要让我决定邀请谁第一个来看这个房子。妈说我有权这样做。"（3—4）

很显然，伊莎贝拉对等级秩序的喜爱，不过是成人世界处世哲学的延伸，在成人世界里，起着主导作用的是财富和资历。正如拥有布偶之屋是真实而具体的，伯纳尔家的长公主对未来权利的梦想也是可以实现的，只是有待时辰。因此，这座玩具房子不仅是伯纳尔庄园所有光鲜的物质财富的一个模拟版本，同时也是一个幻想世界，在这个世界中，羽翼尚嫩的小势利者正准备着正式接管成年势利者的权利。

物质层面的因素是玩偶房子吸引伊莎贝拉的最基本特质。然而，在伯纳尔家中不享有特权的三小姐凯塞娅那里，这却没有多大的吸引力。"布偶爸爸和布偶妈妈"看起来"太僵硬，他们好像在客厅昏倒了似的"（3）。凯塞娅的观察生动地反映出真正的伯纳尔家的父母形象——他们思维僵化，缺乏真诚的感情。凯赛娅还注意到布偶孩子"对布偶房子来说真的太大了"（3），这进一步揭示了她已经意识到自己在家中的状态——这个家对她来说太小了，这里的环境使她精神受制，感觉窒息。真正让她对布偶之屋感到兴奋的是厨房里的那盏小油灯：

> ……凯赛娅真正喜欢、不要命地喜欢的是那盏灯。它摆在餐厅的桌子中间，是个精致的琥珀色的小灯，带着一个白色的灯泡。它装满了油，似乎随时可以用来照明，当然是点不亮的。但里面有些东西看起来像是油，当你摇晃时它就会流动。（3）

凯赛娅喜欢小灯的原因初看起来很简单。和那几个不自然、与环境格格不入的布偶相比，小灯对她来说是"完美的""真实的"、适宜的（3）。人造的布偶讥讽地反映了她的真实生存状态，而这盏在虚假的环境中最"真实"的小灯，却折射了她的幻想世界。

曼斯菲尔德早期作品中意象模式所包含的意义是相对有限而且僵硬的，《布偶之屋》中的小灯则不然，它能使读者产生丰富多元的联想。汉森和格尔对小灯的定义是"艺术"的象征、"是布偶房里所有光鲜的物质背景之下的中心现实"（128）。这样的定义听起来有点模糊，原因有两点：首先，小说的主题是围绕着对生活的直觉而非知性的理解编织而成的；其二是因为小灯是房子中唯一一样能让人憧憬改变的物品，而所有其他东西都是僵硬不变的。德拉尼解释说小灯是"温暖、明亮和安全"的象征，"它使房子成为家"，这对凯赛娅来说尤其如此（12）。这样的解释更符合叙事主题。曼斯菲尔德将僵硬的玩偶和充满生命力的油灯并置，其意图是把以物质价值为核心的中产阶级思维方式和人际关系中真正的爱和温暖作为分化的两极呈现在小说中。

很明显，对凯赛娅来说，伯纳尔庄园与其说是个家，倒不如说是座房子。使她感觉压抑的原因来自两个方面——父母暴君式的统治以及大姐的任性专横。在家中没有人偏爱她，她的声音很难被人听见。伯纳尔家的大人们极少和孩子分享感情，于他们而言，为人父母之责任只粗略地等同于物质上的供给。当凯赛娅斗胆请求母亲允许她邀请被众人孤立的凯尔维姐妹到家里来玩时，她与母亲之间的第一步沟通就遭到了断然拒绝。这种压迫感也延伸至了凯赛娅的学校生活，在学校里，伊莎贝拉几乎在任何场合都比她出彩。

当伊莎贝拉骄傲地向人描述布偶屋里的种种神奇时，凯赛娅说的那句"其中最好的就是那盏灯"的话，几乎没有任何人在听（7）。凯赛娅在家中的地位就相当于凯尔维姐妹在社会中的地位，所以凯尔维姐妹能够自然而然地对小灯带给凯塞娅的感受产生共鸣。

灯有照亮和穿越黑暗的力量，它同时象征着凯赛娅对冷酷现实的觉醒，以及她在想象中超越和重塑现实的力量。如果说布偶之屋的整个场景是充斥着虚伪和势利的成人社会的缩影，那么这盏灯就在孤独地守护着由真和美主宰的童年幻想世界。灯象征着一个孩子对生活的幻想，抗衡着成人世界的错乱和疯狂，这一隐喻含义在《序曲》中也可以看到。在两个故事中，贝莉尔阿姨都不喜欢看见凯赛娅和灯有任何联系，这并非巧合。在《布偶之屋》中，凯赛娅在介绍布偶屋里小灯的美丽之处时，贝莉尔阿姨却赶走了她唯一的听众凯尔维姐妹，粗暴地打断了她的话。在《序曲》中，他们到达新家的那一晚，贝莉尔阿姨几乎是从凯赛娅的手中夺走了灯。正如布偶之屋里的那盏小油灯尽管很吸引人，却不能真的被点燃来使用一样，凯塞娅的幻想也不太可能在冷酷的成人世界中幸存。

这盏小油灯也代表了凯尔维姐妹，即莉尔和埃尔丝的幻想世界，尽管这两个洗衣工女儿的梦想完全是另一码事。如果说凯赛娅只是在家里和学校里遭受冷漠对待，那么凯尔维姐妹无论到哪里都会遭到公开的嘲笑和鄙视。但是凯尔维姐妹能够以几乎和鸵鸟相似的超然态度，来承受着这种社会放逐。曼斯菲尔德将她们描绘成学校里少有的拥有幻想能力的人，这种能力保护她们免受社会歧视的恶意伤害。她们天生的想象力首先体现在她们对大自然的热爱，尽管她们只能买得起"极其普通的花"送给老师。她们具有超常想象力的另一个凭据是：两姐妹之间只需凭直觉而不用语言就能明白彼此的意思：

她（埃尔丝）极少说话。她紧跟在莉尔身后过日子，手里紧捏着莉尔的一角裙子。莉尔去哪，她就跟到哪儿。操场上，或是来往学校的路上，莉尔大步流星走在前头，我们的埃尔丝就紧跟在后。只有在她想要什么东西或是她喘不上气时，我们的埃尔丝才会拽一下莉尔，或是抽一

下胳膊，莉尔就会停下来，转过身。凯尔维姐妹从来也不会误会彼此的意思。(6)

当伊莎贝拉在学校里描绘着玩偶屋里那张了不得的小地毯时，所有其他的女孩子都被迷住了。然而凯尔维姐妹身上的想象力却立刻将她们吸引到了凯赛娅口中的小油灯上。小说结尾处，凯赛娅的话在埃尔丝心中留下了印象。灯的巨大吸引力使凯尔维姐妹克服了恐惧，最终走进伯纳尔家的院子。从故事的最后的一个场景里，我们可以很明显地看出来曼斯菲尔德对凯尔维姐妹的偏爱，因为作为叙事高潮的顿悟时刻，是通过埃尔丝的一声惊叹来实现的——这是我们唯一一次听到她开口：

> ……她们迷迷糊糊地望着干草围场，目光越过小溪，看到了一堆板条，洛根家的奶牛就站在那里等着挤奶。她们在想什么呢？
>
> 现在，我们的埃尔丝微微向前，靠近她的姐姐。现在她已经忘记了那个乖戾的妇人（指贝莉尔）。她伸出一根手指，轻抚她姐姐（帽子上）的那根羽毛；她笑了，非常罕见地笑了。
>
> "我看见那盏灯了"，她轻轻地说。
>
> 她们俩又再次陷入沉默。(12—13)

凯尔维姐妹在面对日常生活的丑陋和残酷之时，依旧还能够欣赏生活的超然之美，这便彰显出他们在精神上超越了学校里那群俗气的女生。凯赛娅和她们的联系开启了超越社会等级鸿沟的理解和沟通的可能性。凯赛娅和凯尔维姐妹通过对灯的依恋，表述了"对其他生活可能性的梦想"，这与曼斯菲尔德运用意象表达象征意义的设想相吻合，即这些意象的"功能都旨在反对任何僵硬固定的思想方法"(Fullbrook 128)。

从《一个理想的家庭》到《布偶之屋》，我们见证了曼斯菲尔德使用意象的整个发展进程。正如曼斯菲尔德一直认为艺术是"纯粹愿景"一样，其作品中的渐进式发展呼应了她生活愿景的逐渐扩展。在早期实验阶段，她对生活的理解还局限于对与她个人相关的事件和情景的狭隘解释，而且她的幻想世界过于依赖她的个人经历，因而不能反映具有普世意义的真相。由于缺乏丰富的暗示性，她用来构建幻想世界的意象通常是以梦中人物的形式出现的，这些意象相对来说是僵硬的。在《一个理想的家庭》《朱丽叶》和《稚气的事》中，无论是替身母亲形象还是理想的灵魂伴侣，都未给读者留下深远的印象，因为它们都没有成功呈现生活的其他可能性，而这种可能性是构成人类梦想不可或缺的因素。

然而，致命的肺病和愈演愈烈的世界大战很快使她转而进入人类整体命运的角度，来看待她自己所遭受的苦难，她的幻想世界开始从纯粹的个人视角转入更为普世的方向，她所使用的意象模式也作出了相应的转变，走向多样化和复杂化。曼斯菲尔德这一时期完成的作品，尤其是《序曲》和《幸福》，尽管仍然是自白体的，却通过一系列更具暗示性的意象反映了更为广泛的生活观。例如，伯莎在《幸福》中的痛苦源自对理解和爱的渴望，这种渴望既是个人化的，也反映了人类普世的愿望。曼斯菲尔德运用了将女主人公的梦幻世界与外部现实联系在一起的多重意象，比如太阳、月亮和梨树，揭示了人类渴望改变现状的梦想是没有边界的。

这种对生命的深刻理解，或者如伊丽莎白·鲍文（Elizabeth Bowen）所言说的"炽热的凝视"，都不会持续太久，因为"最强烈的愿景就其本质来说是不能持续维系的，它注定是断断续续的"（89—90）。这或许解释了曼斯菲尔德艺术生涯最后阶段里完成的作品质量参差不齐的原因。她的代表作《布偶之屋》和《园会》中对意象的选择兼顾了幻想和现实生活的需求。与此同时，我们也发现一些诸如《苍蝇》那样不太成功的例子。由于她不顾一切地想要写出她的天鹅绝唱，也由于她对象征意义的过度关注，她忽视了意象与它们所赖以生存的叙事语境之间的有机联系，因此导致了幻想世界与现实世界的脱节。

第四章

幻想与叙事结构

一直以来，人们都认为凯瑟琳·曼斯菲尔德的叙事结构是她小说中所呈现的现代性的主要原因。尽管她带来了创新的因素，但她的作品中依旧存在构成传统叙事结构的基本要素。幻想的反复运用在叙事结构上起到了既背离传统也坚持传统的重要作用。

A. L. 巴德尔（A. L. Bader）所著的关于现代短篇小说结构的文章中援引的批评家们的指责，或许能反映出一些读者对曼斯菲尔德作品的感受：

> 他们坚持认为现代短篇小说是缺乏情节的、静态的、零散的、不
> 定形的——通常只是一个人物速写或小插叙，或仅仅是对一个瞬间的报
> 道，或者是对情绪或微妙差别的捕捉描绘——总之，它什么都是，只是
> 没有故事。（40）

接下来，巴德尔通过展示构成叙事结构的三个基本要素，来为现代短篇小说家辩护，这三个要素是：情节的推进，换句话说，是矛盾冲突的推进；由冲突导致的高潮；最后是冲突的化解（40）。但巴德尔认为这种基本模式是可以有"相当大的变数"的，因为

> 情节不一定像公式小说那样是件紧身衣，它只是完整的短篇小说形
> 式中的要素之一。因此，情节可能是小说中的主导元素，但也可以从属
> 于人物、主题或氛围等元素。冲突可能有两种基本类型：一种是人物与
> 有形的障碍作斗争的外部冲突，另一种是人物的内心冲突。另外，何时
> 向读者呈现冲突、在什么程度上让读者在小说开端就了解冲突，这也是

可以有极大变数的。(41)

　　巴德尔总结说:"尽管现代短篇小说的技巧千变万化,但它依旧具备从情节中衍生出来的叙事结构"(45)。这些技巧变化背后的关键特征是"间接性"(43)——间接地引出情节发展、冲突和冲突最终的化解。

　　巴德尔对现代短篇小说艺术的有力辩护大致可以用来评价曼斯菲尔德的叙事结构。曼斯菲尔德的小说创作招致了一些批评,有人认为她的作品"**没头没尾**",因为她的开篇总是"**扑通**一声,将人类处境抛入读者的意识中",然后就"无影无踪地退出了",全然不顾矛盾是否得到化解 (Ward 286)。这种评论显然把构成叙事结构的基本要素和表现这些要素的技巧混淆了。从她的作品集中选读几篇小说能帮助我们发现一种结构模式的演变,这种演变被幻想场景所加强,从而印证了巴德尔前面所述的"间接性"理论。

　　情节是叙事结构的主要元素。曼斯菲尔德小说中的情节与传统意义大相径庭。E. M. 福斯特在《小说面面观》(*Aspects of the Novel*)中将情节定义为强调"因果关系的"、按"时间顺序"排列的"事件的叙述"(93)。而罗伯特·斯考尔斯(Robert Scholes)和罗伯特·凯洛格(Robert Kellogg)则认为情节是"叙述中动态的、有顺序的元素"。他们进一步指出"只要人物或叙事文学中任何其他因素变成动态了,它们就都是情节的一部分"(207)。不管他们的定义有何区别,他们都承认行为的进展和时间上的顺序是形成情节的两个必要元素。然而在曼斯菲尔德的小说中,随着幻想元素的加入,情节从由具体行为组成的外部世界转向主观内心世界,叙事行为可以仅仅是一系列的心理过程。因此,包含和反映行为的时间概念也发生了变化。在传统小说中,完成一个行为需要一段按逻辑顺序排列的相对持续的时间,而在曼斯菲尔德的作品中,一个可能超越了时空界限的心理过程,往往只需一眨眼的工夫就能完成。

　　尽管表面上似乎背离了传统,但情节的基本特征之一,即叙事行为的进展,却仍旧保留了下来,只是随着时空的转换,其表现形式变得间接了。《布瑞尔小姐》("Miss Brill")是曼斯菲尔德在情节创新方面非常有启迪性的一篇作品。读者唯一能看到的"行为"，只是一位年迈的老处女在公园走来走去，以及她如何处置一件皮草的情景。看得出来，曼斯菲尔德几乎完全没想在这些细节上做什么铺陈。与传统读者的期望相反，本应由"行为"占主导地位的主要叙事部分，却让位给了女主人公对自己在社交聚会中的吸引力和重要性的连篇幻想。情节不再像传统小说所要求的那样依赖于行为的进展和最终完成，而是通过一个从高度期望跌入深度幻灭的完整心理循环过程展开的。这个循环始于女主人公巨大而虚幻的欣喜感，因为她觉得自己是"人生大舞台上"的一名"演员"（*The Garden Party and other Stories* 204—205），但她最后痛苦地发现：在年轻人的世界里她只是个"愚蠢的老东西"（206）。

在曼斯菲尔德的小说里，幻想在冲突的建构中——巴德尔认为这个建构过程是叙事结构的第二个组成部分——也起着至关重要的作用。由于幻想的干预，情节从由行为构成的客观世界转换到充满心理过程的主观世界。尽管也运用了一些暗示性的细节，但故事冲突主要还是通过主人公的心理过程来铺陈的。由于曼斯菲尔德作品中的大多数角色都不以"行为"为主导，所以与命运的博弈必须在人类心灵的狭小范围内进行。但这种内化并未改变叙事冲突的本质，即人类的崇高理想和龌龊的现实之间存在的普世性的差异，尽管由于幻想场景的加入，冲突的处理方式变得不那么直接了。

曼斯菲尔德的叙事通常以现实和幻想世界表面上的相安无事为开端。当现实世界开始冲击幻想世界时，这个平衡渐渐被打破。当二者发生公开对峙时，叙事就达到了高潮。她的许多小说，尤其是那些触及成长主题的，都是按照这个结构模式创作的。《她的第一次舞会》（"Her First Ball"）是对作者自身青春期经历的一次变相改编，它正好落入了上述的范畴。随着故事的铺开，两条平行但各自独立的线索逐渐形成，一条是薛立丹家的乡下表亲莱拉所代表的对永恒青春和美丽的梦想，另一条则是由一个"穷酸的""衰老的"男人所代表的生命短暂无常的冷酷现实（*The Garden Party and Other Stories* 216）。这两条线索之间不可避免的冲突，是通过老男人和莱拉作为舞伴在舞会上的相遇来展示的。他在跳舞时对她说："你不能希望任何事情会持续这么久，绝不会的，过不了多久你就会坐在舞台上，穿着你漂亮的黑色天鹅绒裙子，看着别人跳舞。这漂亮的手臂会变得又短又粗"（217）。这短短的一句话开启了莱拉对生老概念的最初意识，因而粉碎了她年轻的幻想。她歇斯底地叫嚷着"我想要停下来"（218），由此引入了叙事的高潮。就这样，在幻想元素的协助下，故事主题的发展（即莱拉的知识经验启蒙过程）与叙事冲突所形成的结构进展达成了重合。

在叙事结构中，矛盾化解通常紧跟在高潮冲突之后。曼斯菲尔德小说的终结方式引起了一些评论家的不满，他们认为她的结尾过于突兀，有时也缺乏铺陈，因为这样的结尾没有提供化解危机的合理方案。评论家们觉得这样的结局既不能延展也不能终止叙事冲突，只能表明作家缺乏全面的结构设想。这类批评通常是由于批评家对"冲突的化解"的狭义解释所造成的。在叙事行为和冲突都发生在人类的内心领域的这类故事中，冲突的化解因而可以运用"感知时刻"来体现（Bader 43）。由于危机是建立在幻想和现实之间的差异之上的，因此解决当下冲突的关键，在于人物发现并认识到作为幻想对立面而存在的客观真相。当叙事达到这个认知点时，内心的争战就会随着幻想世界的渐行渐远而暂告终结。这也许就是巴德尔所说的"通过间接暗示……得到解决"的意思（43）。

在曼斯菲尔德的故事中，冲突的化解有两种基本方式。在第一种方式中，主观真理或者说幻想的小世界在与客观现实的对抗中彻底破灭；主人公在经历了期望的反转之后暂时迷失了方向，但最终却因获得对生活的新认知而重新找到方向。《园会》中的劳拉就是如此。在第二种方式中，主要人物承受住了幻想破灭带来的冲击，因为他们或是将幻想转化为了积极的因素，或是重塑了一个新的幻想世界。具有代表性的两个例子就是《她的第一次舞会》和《布偶之屋》。

由于冲突的化解对任何主题完整的小说都至关紧要，所以"顿悟的重要时刻"（Madden 5504A）在曼斯菲尔德的叙事结构中就显得尤其关键。曼斯菲尔德本人在发布以下评论的时候，就已敏锐地意识到了这一点：

　　因此，危机是我们"中心要点"的最重要因素，营造危机的企图和

139

情感是我们靠近或远离它的旅程中所经历的阶段。正如我们所看到的那样，如果没有危机，小说的形式就会消失。假如没有危机，我们如何才能理解这一个"精神事件"有别于那一个的重要性呢？——假如成长和启蒙过程的铺陈并没有导致一个燃烧的刹那，我们怎样才能防止这些事件失去关联——尽管其自身是完整的呢？（*Novels and Novelists* 29—30）

这个"燃烧的刹那"是指作品中的人物突然获得新的生命感悟的那个时刻。曼斯菲尔德围绕着这个重要的顿悟时刻编织出她的"逃离与受陷"母题（Madden 5504A），以此展示现实与幻想的互动过程。这些方法大致可以归入凯瑟琳·休姆的"愿景文学"技巧分类之中，休姆认为"愿景文学"是帮助"虚构的世界"来"评论现实世界"的（83）。根据休姆的分析研究，这些技巧被分成三大类：增强型，削弱型和对比型。休姆认为：在"增强型"中，愿景或幻想中呈现的世界"比我们日常的现实显得更充实、更丰富、更多彩和生动，或者…… 它提醒我们，我们自身世界中存在着许多被我们在无意识中错过的内容"。用"削减型"技巧构建的世界要么是"基于对现实非常狭隘的解释"，在这个世界里"人类经验的很大部分"被排除在外；要么是"作者故意删除了该有的素材，特别是行为之间的那些逻辑联系"。第三种技巧是"削减型之下的一个特殊子类，它创造出互为观照的世界"，"将现实的复杂性细化成两个兴趣点，这两者之间的紧张关系构成了对现实本质的评判"（83）。休姆对愿景文学的评论，为曼斯菲尔德创作艺术的研究指出了方向，因为曼斯菲尔德的小说中运用幻想来强化叙事结构的各种技巧，大致上产生了休姆所预测的效果。

休姆所说的增强型或添加型的幻想模式在曼斯菲尔德的作品中反复出现过，尤其是在那一系列发生在作者神秘的故国新西兰、以伯纳尔和薛立丹家族为中心的小说中。在那篇旨在成为《序曲》续篇的小说《在海湾》（"At the Bay"）中，曼斯菲尔德将这个技巧运用到几近完美的地步。

《序曲》和《在海湾》中各种五花八门事件的松散联系，引发了评论界对小说整体结构设计的批评。马文·马格拉纳在《凯瑟琳·曼斯菲尔德的小说》

（*The Fiction of Katherine Mansfield*）中和其他评论家一样表达了他的困惑：

> 在《在海湾》中，曼斯菲尔德比在《序曲》中更加疯狂地漠视当代评
> 论家的要求，即一件艺术作品要有紧凑的结构、其专题框架的每个部分
> 都应彼此连接顺畅。（《在海湾》中）每个情节与其他情节的相关性并不
> 总是明晰的，这个相关性在某些情况下之所以没能显示出来，是因为除
> 了一些朦胧模糊的表现方式之外，它本身根本就不存在。（39）

虽然乍一看，在《在海湾》中，叙事结构并没有清晰的呈现，但它依旧
有着自身的严密性，尽管这种严密性是与传统叙述方法相悖的。构成叙事主
体的十二个故事大部分都是结构完整、自成一体的。当个别故事本身就包含
了或是直叙或是暗示的行为、冲突和冲突化解时，它们结合在一起形成了一
个更大的统一主题，即曼斯菲尔德作品中反复出现的逃离和受陷的母题。这
些故事不是通过明显的逻辑，而是通过一个由幻想和现实交替统治的统一时
空框架联系在一起的。这十二个故事按同心模式安排，以新月湾为轴心，以
二十四小时的时间段为圆周。马格拉纳的困惑并不能完全解释得通，因为在
这里，曼斯菲尔德这位更有想法的现代作家，已经把填补缺失逻辑关联的繁
重任务，留给了她那些更为成熟的现代读者。

《在海湾》是一篇有争议的小说。例如，切丽·汉金就坚持认为它比《序
曲》更优秀，因为

> 凯瑟琳·曼斯菲尔德现在需要探索的还不是人类关系的神秘深
> 度，而是生活本身的神秘起落。她必须要把她独自面对的死亡放到更
> 广泛、更普遍的角度来看待——用这样的角度来看待所有自然形态的
> 死亡——还有重生。因此，在《在海湾》这篇小说中，个人的痛苦和遗
> 憾都需要让位给人类因意识到生命的短暂而产生的普遍和共通的痛苦。
> （*Confessional Stories* 223）

更广泛、更深刻的主题需要有更复杂的叙事结构来承载。由于复杂的人际关系已经渐渐淡出显著的位置，主题冲突和由此产生的叙事高潮开始集中体现在"惰性"和"探索"的两极分化上（Hankin *Confessional Stories* 231），曼斯菲尔德的主要小说人物按照这两个群体进行了划分和重组。具有讽刺意味的是，这两种基本生活态度之间的分歧，却源于他们对生命无常的共同认识。人物按照懒散或活跃清晰地分成了两个阵营，但他们通常都用幻想来拓展他们在现实生活中有限的可能性。

惰性与探索之间的冲突，很早就通过诸如琳达、贝莉尔、斯坦利和乔纳森等人物所持的人生哲学展现了出来。和《序曲》中一样，《在海湾》中的琳达仍然对自己的妻子与母亲的角色心怀怨恨，但现在她的痛苦被一丝淡淡的幽默感所稀释了：

> 偶尔会有片刻的平静的喘息瞬间，但其余的时间里都像是住在一座无可救药地习惯性失火的房子里或是一艘每天都失事的船上一样。而且斯坦利总是处于险境的核心。琳达所有时间都花在拯救他、让他复原、使他平静下来以及听他讲故事上。假若还有她还有时间剩下来，那就都用在了对付生儿育女的恐惧上。（*The Garden Party and Other Stories* 33）

在认识到生命的脆弱之后，琳达对毫无意义的日常生活的怨恨变得更为尖锐。当她一边看着花园里的花朵绽放，一边"在梦幻中虚度清晨"时，一种最根本的无助感悄然爬上心头（30）：

> 要是一个人有足够长的时间观赏这些花，有足够长的时间克服新奇和陌生感，有足够长的时间来认识它们就好了！但是，只要他一停下来拨开花瓣去观看叶子的背面，生命就会扑面而来将他席卷而去。琳达躺在藤椅上，感到自己是如此的轻，轻得像是一片叶子。生命如风一般吹来，琳达被这风抓住了，被震撼了。她不得不离开。哦，亲爱的，会一直这样吗？无人能逃得过去吗？（32）

此时，琳达想要摆脱妻子和母亲这两个她不愿承担的角色的个人愿望，让位给了人类想要逃避死亡控制的普遍欲望。她和斯坦利之间始于《序曲》的冲突，现在已经超越了性的狭隘界限，延伸到他们对生活本身的态度上。小说中她的懒散态度蕴意深远，其中包含了节省生命支出的意味。于她而言，参与任何实质性的体力活动就是犯下了消耗体能的罪。而正是家务琐事、预期的性义务以及最糟糕的生育创痛这些事，在缩减着原本已经有限的寿命。

与琳达的懒散相反的是斯坦利的活跃。同样意识到生命的短暂，他积极地利用每一分钟来与日趋逼近的死亡阴影抗衡，他的整个存在都是由身体的行为所定义的——工作、运动、吃饭和纵欲。斯坦利在这里扮演的角色比《序曲》中那个简单的性爱狂魔更为过分，现在他的存在就是对琳达生存意识的直接威胁。

琳达身体上的懒散似乎同时对照并加速了她的精神活动，她实际上是小说中沉陷得最深的一个幻想家。她的幻想包括一系列内容宽泛的体验，这些体验拓展了她有限的现实生存状态。例如，她可以通过重拾童年的探索梦想，来补偿她缺乏任何实质性活动的生活现状：

> ……她现在坐在塔斯马尼亚的家的阳台上，靠在父亲的膝盖上。他对她承诺道："琳妮，等你和我的年纪都足够大的时候，我们就跑到哪个地方去，我们会逃走的。像两个男孩一样。我都能看到我在中国的一条河上航行呢。"琳达看见了那条河，它很宽，到处泊满了木筏和小船。她看见了船夫们的黄帽子，听见了他们高亢尖锐的号子声……（32）

从这里我们可以看见，惰性和探索之间的冲突不仅体现在琳达与斯坦利爱恨交织的关系上，也体现在她对冒险的幻想和一成不变的婚姻生活之间的差异上。她与斯坦利的冲突并没恶化到完全破裂的地步，这倒不是如汉金试图说服我们的那样（*Confessional Stories* 233），因为琳达"重新发现了她对他的爱"并"接受他的种种缺陷"，而是因为琳达意识到了：人类所付出的任何抗争，在无坚不摧不可规避的生命法则面前都是无足轻重的。她之所以能够接受现实，也部分受益于幻想对现实的补足和扩充功能，因为幻想使她更全面地理解了她受限的现实。琳达承认受挫，因而使叙事冲突得到了化解，因为幻灭"给我们的心态和世界观带来了强大的挑战"，它"让我们想起了我们的自由"（Hume 126）。

在琳达和她儿子的关系中也会出现这样的顿悟时刻。在现实生活中，她无法与斯坦利就儿子／继承人所产生的那种骄傲感产生共鸣，但在幻想中，这个男孩的出现丰富了她对生活本质的理解。在《序曲》的第六个故事中，琳达沉浸在清晨的幻想中，和这个孩子进行着一场想象中的心灵对话，孩子对生活的直觉信念激起她心中一股尖锐的爱意：

> 琳达对这个小东西的自信感到很惊讶……啊，不，真诚点吧，这不是她感受到的。她感受到的是完全不同的东西，是从未有过的新鲜感觉，如此的……她泪眼婆娑。她轻轻地向男孩呢喃道："你好啊，我的小逗宝！"（35）

此处，幻想的运用再次化解了主题的冲突。由于琳达认识到了生命代谢的必然性，她最终接受了这个男孩并且爱上了他。但她的这些认识并不是通过每天与现实的接触得来的，而是在幻想中异想天开的时刻里顿悟到的。从幻想的角度来看，婴儿不再是威胁、缩减她生命的一种邪恶力量，而是她自身存在的一种延续和重生。

在《在海湾》中，主题的主要冲突基本是通过琳达对斯坦利和孩子们的矛盾态度铺展开来的，而其他人物如贝莉尔·费尔菲尔德和乔纳森·屈劳特也被卷入冲突的漩涡。他们渴望冒险，但是他们预期的社会角色却阻挡他们去冒险，他们在这两者中间苦苦挣扎。在复杂的伯纳尔家庭框架中，贝莉尔站在姐姐琳达和姐夫斯坦利中间，同时分享着前者做白日梦的习惯和后者对身体活动的热衷。探索与惰性的冲突在她身上体现为：她一方面热切地沉湎于幻想中的情感冒险，一方面又害怕白日梦会最终威胁并替代现实。就像在《序曲》中那样，贝莉尔"只有一条通往幸福的路"——那就是体面的婚姻（Fullbrook 112），因为她的整个社会身份都是通过获取一个丈夫来确定的。和琳达一样，贝莉尔把自己裹在幻想中，幻想是对她那贫乏的情感生活的补充，也是唯一一条她可以梦想着靠自己的努力获取社会认可的途径。在海滩上与肯伯太太进行了一天的探险之后，她与灌木丛展开了一场想象中的对话，透露出她渴望有一个幻想情人帮助她迅速从生活危机中解脱出来的心境：

　　"把我从这些人身边带走吧，我的爱人。让我们远走高飞。让我们过自己的生活，全新的、自己的生活，一切从头开始。让我们生起属于自己的篝火吧。让我们俩一起坐下来吃东西。让我们晚上促膝长谈吧。"
　　她当时的想法几乎就是"亲爱的，救救我。救救我吧！"（63）

　　她和肯伯一家的关系是她的幻想世界的延伸。理查德·F·彼得森（Richard F. Peterson）在《真理的圈子》（"The Circle of Truth"）一文中错误地认为：这篇小说主要的"干扰或缺陷"来自家族圈子之外。他认为"曼斯菲尔德把肯伯家族引入到伯纳尔家族的生存模式中，这种做法营造了一种黑暗和威胁的氛围……并使人物的人生观与《序曲》中变得有所不同"（389）。其实以伯纳尔家庭为中心的叙事结构，并没有因为贝莉尔与肯伯一家的冒险行动而变得松散，他们的介入反而给既定的生活秩序添加了一个新的维度。这同时也加剧了主题冲突的效果，因为它揭示了贝莉尔对探索所持的既热爱又恐惧的矛盾心情。他们的关系构成了贝莉尔奇异的性幻想的一个组成部分，但当幻想威胁着要取代而不是扩宽现实时，她很快就抽身而退。在小说的最后一幕里，她退缩着没有与哈利·肯伯产生亲昵接触，这一行为代表着"她逃避了自身的欲望和满足，同时也逃避了为自我认同而陷入的扭曲婚姻"（Fullbrook 113）。
　　琳达身上的惰性的起因来自她的婚姻生活，但贝莉尔对行动的渴望却源于改变现状（即寻找婚姻机遇）的愿望。因此，当主题冲突围绕着她们对生活基本看法的分歧展开时，琳达眼里的束缚就成了贝莉尔获取自由的途径。

贝莉尔的紧张和危机的化解也取决于她对挫折和失败的认知。当她匆忙逃离可憎的哈利·肯伯的怀抱时，就已经表明她认识到了幻想是不足以替代现实的。冲突被含蓄地化解之后，宁静的秩序得到了暂时的恢复，这标志着叙事的结束。小说结尾时再次提到了大海，只是此时它却处于夜晚的宁静之中：

> 一片小小的宁静的云朵从月亮前飘过。在天阴下来的那一刻，大海听起来很遥远、很苦恼。然后云朵飞走了，大海的声音变成了一种模糊不清的低语，仿佛它刚从噩梦中醒了似的。一切都寂静无声。（67）

如果《在海湾》中，幻想是通过对现实的补充来达到结构的完整性，那么它在《布瑞尔小姐》中的主要作用，却是通过强化女主人公有限的生活愿景，然后证明它是完全错误的，以此建立起故事的张力。显而易见，这两篇小说的总体结构设计是大相径庭的，前者是"根据象征模式的要求"以片段的形式构建的（Hanson and Gurr 76），而后者则更加紧密地遵循行为、时间和空间的统一规则。结构性差异不只是由于叙事单元，或者说情景事件的不同安排而导致的，它也与幻想进入叙事的不同方式以及对主题造成的不同影响有关。

用休姆的标准来衡量，布瑞尔小姐在幻想中编造的那个世界是个经过了"削减"的世界。她的幻想往往更倾向于使用非常狭隘的概念来定义生活，这样的幻想不仅没有丰富和扩展她的视野，反而"忽略了大部分的人类经验"（Hume 83）。布瑞尔小姐是个贫穷的、年迈的社会边缘人，她靠一种神经质的、梦幻似的想象力存活，认为自己的存在对他人的生活至关重要。我们在《在海湾》中所发现的静止与活力、幻想与现实之间的主题冲突，在这篇小说里延伸到了"衰老与年轻""孤独与归属"的对立上（Hanson and Gurr 77）。由于故事完全是从女主人公的意识角度叙述的，直到接近结尾处，读者才清晰地感受到了故事冲突，因为布瑞尔小姐直到那时才发现：自己梦幻般的期待和无情的现实之间存在着一条巨大的鸿沟。

布瑞尔小姐虚幻的生活观念和她那虚假的社会归属感共同构成了主要

叙事冲突。她狭隘地认为：一个人的存在仅仅由青春的容颜、活力和社会的接纳所定义。她对那条寒酸的皮裘领子的痴迷，便是她狭隘心态的一个表现——那对她来说是一种生命的象征：

> 可爱的小东西！再次触摸到它真是太好了。那天下午她把它从盒子里拿了出来，抖掉上面的防蛀粉，好好地刷了一遍，把灰暗的小眼睛擦得又有了元气。"我怎么了？"那双悲伤的小眼睛问道。哦，见到那双眼睛从陈货里走出来重新又瞪着她看，真是太好了…… 小流氓！是的，她真的是这么想的。小流氓就在她的左耳旁边咬着自己的尾巴。她本可以把它摘下来，放在她的腿上然后抚摸它的，可她的手和手臂都感到一阵麻，但她想，那是走路造成的。（*The Garden Party and Other Stories* 199-200）

皮裘在幻想中被拟人化了，这揭示了标题女主人公对生活的过分解读和不知所措。她明显不愿去修复皮裘破损的鼻子，除非到"万不得已的时候"（200），这就将她不愿意面对逝去青春的内心活动进一步外在化。她需要外在物件和人群的支撑来确认自己的存在，这也是她为何经常去公园的原因所在。

随着布瑞尔小姐来到公共花园欣赏音乐会并偷听游人们的对话，幻想持续地在叙事中占据着主导地位。她幻想着自己的重要性，她觉得整个场景是个巨大的舞台，而她自己则是个不可忽略的女演员：

> 哦，真是太吸引人了！她多么享受啊！她多么喜欢坐在那里看着这一切！这就像一出戏。确确实实就像一出戏……他们都在舞台上。他们不仅仅是观众，不仅仅在观看，他们是在演戏。就连她都有个角色，每个礼拜天都到场。毫无疑问，如果她没到场的话，一定会有人注意到的。毕竟，她是戏里的一个角儿。（204）

她对活力和友谊的错误理解预示并加剧了小说高潮的冲突，这个冲突是推迟到叙事结尾时才出现的。公园游人之间彼此的漠不关心和格格不入并未引起她的注意，在她的奇妙想象中，她觉得这些在人生舞台上来来往往忙忙碌碌的人，都和她有着因共同经历而生出的情谊。当真正的男女主角进入"剧场"，并明确表示出对她的厌恶时，这种幻觉的表皮终于被撕扯了下来：

> 女孩说："不行，现在不行，这儿不行，我不能。"
>
> 男孩问："这是为什么啊？是因为那头那个老蠢货吗？她究竟为什么到这儿来——谁要看她呢？她为什么不把她那张愚蠢的老脸留在家里呢？"（206）

在这里，"从虚幻的快乐中灾难性跌落"（Daly 90）的效果被大大加强了，首先，因为它是从布瑞尔小姐自己的视角中揭示的；其次，因为它彻底击碎了那个对她来说意味着全部生存意义的幻想世界。当她无意中听到那场对话时，她终于意识到自己的存在，或者说任何一个人的存在，对整个人类社会而言都是无足轻重的。这顿悟的时刻预示着重大的主题冲突得到了化解，因为女主人公在经历幻想破灭之后，讽刺性地重新找回了面对残酷的孤独生活的勇气，此时紧张的气氛暂时得到了缓解。她不再假装她还年轻以博得众人的注意，而是急急忙忙地回到了家，这时的她，已经不是先前的那个她了：

> 她在那儿坐了很久。装皮裘的盒子就在床上。她迅速地打开毛皮领的锁扣，非常迅速、一眼也没看就把它放进了盒子里。但当她盖上盒盖时，她仿佛听到什么东西在哭泣。（207）

从隐喻的意义来说，在昏暗孤独的房间里被布瑞尔小姐关进盒子里去的并不是那块裘皮领子，而是她对生活的美好梦想。随着盒子的关闭，她也告别了她的那个幻想世界。她突然发现自己身上有了渐渐强大的坚韧和尊严感，她已经做好准备来面对这个令人不快的孤独现实。然而，这一高潮时刻和随之到来的冲突化解却被一丝做作感毁坏了。如同在《序曲》里一样，虽然人物对生活的幻想能够激起读者的同情和哀伤，但是在这里现实却显得是经过"人工安排"的，给人留下"持久印象"的"不是生活，而是作者本身的小聪明"（Peterson 385）。

　　幻想在《布瑞尔小姐》的叙事框架中起的是"删减"作用，但在曼斯菲尔德的杰作《园会》中，它却形成了对立叙事的两极之一。这个故事的主要冲突是围绕着两个关注极点展开的——一个是上流社会的薛立丹家庭及其流金溢彩的社交场合，另一个是极为贫穷的社区和一个可怜车夫的悲惨死亡。批评家们有时过分强调了死亡在这篇小说中的重要性，把它视为主题结构的中心。这样的解读明显曲解了曼斯菲尔德自己的原意，她宣称她旨在描绘"生命的多样性以及我们如何尝试融入一切，**包括死亡**"（Letters 454；强调为引者所加）。虽然从隐喻的角度来说，可怜的车夫的死亡在年轻女主人公从无知到认知的途程中起着绝对的里程碑式的作用，但小说主要的关注点还是在"生活的恩惠和生存的耻辱"上（Hormasji 115）。

　　在曼斯菲尔德的许多小说中，叙事行为主要由一些一闪而过的顿悟时刻组成，《园会》的主题冲突是围绕着薛立丹家的社交聚会展开的，事件中牵涉的不仅有内在的心理活动，也有外在的身体活动。薛立丹一家代表着欢乐与辉煌的梦幻世界，而斯科特一家则显示了现实中不堪入目的另一面，二者之间的分界线既是具体的，也含有隐喻意义。导致该小说高潮冲突的对立两极，本质上都是建立在时间、空间和氛围的差异上的，这些差异把这两个世界区分开来。

　　叙事开始于薛立丹全家为园会所做的一系列准备工作上。薛立丹一家习惯性地沉迷于幻想中，这在他们安排聚会的方式中直接显现了出来。曼斯菲尔德描绘他们家花园的语气，表明了她对薛立丹一家生活方式的嘲讽。很显然，这个花园并不像安德斯·艾弗森（Anders Iversen）在《读凯瑟琳·曼斯菲尔德〈园会〉有感》（"A Reading of Katherine Mansfield's 'The Garden Party'"）一文中所说的，是个完美的"超越时空界限""富足自然"的天堂（8—9）。梦幻般的人造感充溢着他们家的每个角落，在那里人们可以按照计划"订购"

大自然并把大自然安排得秩序井然（*The Garden Party and Other Stories* 68）。精心布置的草坪、鲜花和帐篷，只是他们改装自然环境的一部分，唯一的目的是要给人留下深刻的印象。

这种人造感是薛立丹一家的幻想世界里的一个组成部分，它还体现在劳拉在与工人交谈时试图模仿她母亲的语气、乔斯指令仆人时效仿她父母的姿势，以及她唱那首"生活多么**厌——烦**，/ 希望终究要死亡，/ 梦境总是会**醒——来**"这首歌时，用夸张的拖腔演绎伤感之情上（77）。

这种充斥着人造感的环境破坏了表面的自然和活力，使一切落在其间的事物都变得虚幻起来。从结构的角度来看，那些描述薛立丹一家对园会的梦幻期待的长篇大论，都旨在让读者做好准备进入作为对应两极的另一极的生活之中，真正的危机正暗藏在这种幸福生活的表层之下。劳拉作为薛立丹家中"有艺术天赋的那一个"（69），比他人更具备幻想能力。她运用想象力，把墨水壶盖上的"小小的阳光斑点"变成了"一颗温暖的小银星"（74）。她以同样的想象力，把那些来家里搭帐篷的工人浪漫地设想成"落难王子"（71—72）。

于是，在她的多愁善感的情绪里，"比常人更低贱"的工人，现在变成了"超越常人的人"（Iversen 11）。尽管她自欺欺人地认为：她"一丢丢"都不在意"这些荒谬的阶级区分"（72），但她还是忍不住用居高临下的姿态和他们说话，试图表现出她"看上去很严肃，甚至有点近视"（69）；她还犹豫不定，不知道"一个工人和她谈到垂到眼睛里的刘海是否合乎体统"（70）。劳工阶层对她的吸引力更多地是由新鲜感所触发的，而这种新鲜感是她备受呵护的蝴蝶般的生活所产生的自然结果。但随着情节的急剧转变，她的多愁善感立刻被一刀斩断。

第一个叙述高潮（尽管是虚假的）发生在工人出事的消息传到正在厨房的劳拉那里时。她从幸福的巅峰一下子坠入了深深的困惑中。然而这个粉碎性的时刻是瞬间即逝的，因为她当时只是被死亡的传闻所震惊而已。死亡的消息和家人对此的冷漠无情，激发了她的悲哀和愤慨，但这种情绪很快就被对园会的期待所模糊了：

　　只是一瞬间，她眼前又闪现出那个可怜的女人和那些孩子，还有那具尸体被抬进屋里的情景。但一切似乎都是模糊的，不真实的，就像报纸上的一张照片。等园会完了我再来想这件事吧。她对自己说。这似乎是个最好的办法……（84）

　　当劳拉决定顺从于幻想时，贫穷和死亡这令人不快的事实就变成了"模糊"和"不真实"的背景，而精心设计的园会于她而言仍然是唯一有形的现实。虽然薛立丹家所有的女性都爱沉湎于幻想，但是如果这种沉湎有走向极端的危险时，她们就会联合一致来抵抗它。例如，当事故发生时，劳拉曾一度冲动地想终止园会，但被母亲和姐妹们一致谴责为"荒谬"和"奢侈"（84）。对她们来说，想象力和荒谬之间只隔着一条细线，"人物可以从一个被社区全然接纳的成员，轻而易举地瞬间坠落为一个绝对的被放逐者"（Fullbrook 123）。

　　第一次叙述高潮是关于幸福的幻想和死亡逼近的阴影之间的冲突，紧接着的第二次高潮冲突发生在劳拉被迫走出家门面对真实的死亡之时——这个行程具备字面和隐喻的双重意义。直到小说篇幅接近五分之四时，叙事结构中对立两极中的另一极，即劳工邻居们所栖身的黑暗世界，才被引进了读者的视线。

　　当这两个世界的对照变得越来越明显时，劳拉去往斯科特家的途程便不再仅仅是一次身体意义上的活动，它含有了更多心理层面的意义。这位年轻女主人公没心没肺的幸福感已经被死亡的模糊传闻所污染。当她离开她那人造的富庶的花园，进入工人居住区昏暗的小巷时，幸福感已经逐渐让位给忧虑甚至恐惧：

　　现在已经穿过了这条宽阔的路，进入了小巷。小巷烟雾浓重，很是幽暗。身穿披肩和戴着男人粗呢帽的妇女们匆匆走过。男人醉趴在栅栏上，孩子们在门口玩耍。从这些丑陋的小屋里传出低沉的嘤嗡声。有些小屋里透出一丝亮光，螃蟹似的影子爬过窗户。劳拉低下头，急急忙忙地往前赶。她现在真希望她穿着一件外套。她的连衣裙太惹眼了！还有那顶饰有天鹅绒飘带的大帽子——要是换一顶别的帽子就好了！人们在看她吗？他们一定在看。来这里真是个错误的决定……（89）

这种对比不仅是空间上的而且还是时间上的。清晨时，劳拉和她的姐妹们正怀着热切的期待为园会做着准备。而当劳拉走向斯科特家时，"完美的下午"已经"慢慢熟了，慢慢凋谢"，它的"花瓣闭合了"（86）。这条小巷是个黄昏的世界，它将苦难、悲伤和死亡的认知注入劳拉的意识之中。正如亚当·索尔金（Adam J. Sorkin）敏锐地指出的那样，死亡的"陌生感"是导致她过度反应的原因：

> 正是富裕生活带来的特殊心理影响模糊了贫困和死亡的冲击，把死亡推到一个距离之外，并将之仪式化，让死亡听起来像是别处——肯定是从（就像故事里所说的）虚幻的天堂般的花园之外——传来的不同寻常的消息。（446）

真正的叙事高潮发生在故事结尾处劳拉与死亡产生面对面的接触时。但是正如马格拉纳所述，劳拉并没通过"接触死亡"而"从她的梦幻生活，即园会以及薛立丹家独有的奢华之中清醒过来"（*The Fiction of Katherine Mansfield* 117）。尽管她感到震惊和困惑，匆忙地接受了死亡的存在，但死亡对她来说不属于现实，而只是梦幻的一部分。因此，死去的车夫在她的幻想中被浪漫地想象成另一个王子：

> 那个年轻人躺在那里，睡得很香，睡得很沉，离他们两人都很遥远。哦，如此遥远，如此宁静。他在做梦。永远不要叫醒他。他的头陷在枕头里，眼睛紧闭；眼睛在闭合的眼皮底下什么也看不见。他向梦妥协了。园会、食品篮子、饰有花边的连衣裙和他有什么关系呢？……他很好，长得也好看……幸福……幸福……这张沉睡的脸在说一切都安

好无恙。（91—92）

通过幻想，劳拉可以缓解死亡带给她的震惊，但现在她的幻想里已经有了一个更宽广的维度。当她回到薛立丹家中的花园时，她已经不是同一个女孩了，她变得比以前明智了，因为她已经部分摆脱了这个虚幻天堂的狭隘思维方式，她对生命有了新的认知，这个新认知里包括了对死亡的意识。尽管她还无法解释这一新认知的具体含义，但这个认知却标志着劳拉走向成人的第一步，同时也暂时化解了成长的痛苦带来的张力。薛立丹家所代表的世界和斯科特家代表的世界之间的矛盾，得到了相对的协调，而协调这二者的，正是劳拉对美的真诚赞赏，这种赞赏跨越了两个世界之间的巨大鸿沟。正如劳拉对生活的新认知是用含蓄而不是明示的方式表述的，叙事冲突的化解也是采用了同样的手法。

综上所述，从《在海湾》《布瑞尔小姐》《园会》等多篇小说中，我们可以发现一种相对一致的叙事模式，这种模式是以幻想为手段来加强小说结构的。那些认为曼斯菲尔德作品"无结构"的指责并不完全合理，因为在其作品中，构成叙事结构的最基本要素，即行为、冲突和冲突的化解都依然存在，只不过表现方式不同而已。虽然幻想带来了时间和空间概念的创新解读，并将情节、冲突和冲突化解转入了个体的心理范畴，但由于叙事行为和冲突的本质保持不变，人物和事件仍然是动态的。

正如我们在前面讨论过的小说中发现的那样，从结构角度来看，曼斯菲尔德作品中幻想的主要功能是对结构形成增强、削减或对比作用。在"增强"功能中，作者在情节中引入了幻想以拓宽主人公有限的人生体验。人物在对白日梦的热爱和对幻想取代现实的恐惧之间摇摆不定，而叙事冲突就是围绕着这两极展开的。冲突的化解途径要么是人物在被幻想所拓充的世界中获得了暂时的满足感，要么是人物公开承认自己的沮丧和失败，就像《在海湾》中的琳达和贝莉尔那样。

在"削减"功能中，幻想进入叙事场景的方式是将女主人公的视角缩小成对生活非常排他的解读。当现实突然闯入并最终粉碎了这个排他的世界时，叙事冲突就被演化为高潮的冲突。这些高潮时刻之后通常跟随着隐而不宣的冲突化解，因为受害者就像《布瑞尔小姐》和《家庭女教师》中的女主人公一样，不能再把幻想作为存在的中流砥柱，她们在无形中被推入了不得不直面赤裸现实的状态。

幻想还可以在与现实的对峙中建立起价值观迥异的对立两极，并通过这两极的对照来强化叙事结构。小说人物被困在两个世界之间，他们的困惑成为情节和叙事冲突的主要部分。正如《园会》和《时髦的婚姻》那样，顿悟时刻并不是因为人物发现了一条能立即化解困惑的途径，而是他们找到了一种能超越既定真理观的新生命哲学。

第五章

结论

　　埃德加·爱伦·坡（Edgar Allan Poe）在讨论短篇小说的艺术时，将"整体效果"单独列为"最重要的一点"。他一直认为没有持续的努力，"人们的心灵永远不会被深深打动"（2）。凯瑟琳·曼斯菲尔德本人也意识到了这个"重要性"，正如她向她的艺术家小叔子理查德·莫里（Richard Murry）坦言的那样，她"热衷……将各种事情汇成一个整体的技巧"（*Letters* 364）。艾琳·巴德斯威勒（Eileen Baldeshwiler）用现代文学批评术语解读这种热衷，认为它其实是对那些"令人眼花缭乱的……与深层意义毫无贡献的细节"的厌恶，这些细节"只会削弱整体效果"（426）。爱伦·坡所指的"持续努力"，在曼斯菲尔德作品中是以反复出现的幻想场景来呈现的。尽管她偶尔也会改变主题和视角，但幻想仍是她一以贯之的特征，是她作品的主题、人物塑造、象征意义以及叙事结构的一个组成部分。从最早期的诸如《一个理想的家庭》和《我的盆栽》等作品，到包含《帕克大妈的一生》和《布偶之屋》在内的绝笔之作，曼斯菲尔德一直都在致力于把幻想当作探索和评论现实本质的一种手段。

　　但是，这种"持续努力"本身并不一定能产生爱伦·坡和曼斯菲尔德都谈到的"整体效果"，或者说艺术"整体"。例如，在她早期作品中，曼斯菲尔德想要通过幻想来反思审视现实的目的就经常被打断甚至扭曲，因为她的女主人公过分沉湎于白日梦。由于虚幻世界不是在评论现实，而是几乎完全遮蔽了实证意义上的现实世界，叙事的"整体效果"或大体印象被稀释了。因此，最初用来实现目的的手段，却于无意中击败了目的。在《一件稚气但十分自然的事》和《家庭女教师》中就能看到这样的例子，其中主人公的幻想世界几乎完全不与他们的现实环境产生联系。

　　然而，在曼斯菲尔德较为成熟的作品中，幻想的运用却是有助于揭示现实的本质的。根据罗伯特·斯科尔斯和罗伯特·凯洛格所说：

> 在一部叙事艺术作品中，意义是以下两个世界之间的关系函数：作者创造的虚幻世界，以及"真实"世界，即我们可以理解的宇宙。当我们说我们"读懂"了某部作品，我们指的是我们在这两个世界之间发现了一种或一组令人满意的关系。（82）

上面所提到的"虚幻"的和"令人满意的"两个词，可以更为恰当地替换为"幻想的"和"启示性的"。在曼斯菲尔德后期的大部分小说中，她通过幻想揭示现实本质的"持续努力"最终产生了"整体效果"，因为她在这两个世界之间建立起了一系列关系，并对这些关系进行了检验。有时，作者通过揭露幻想在模拟现实的环境中的不可实现性，从而将幻想摆在了现实的对立面，《园会》中的劳拉幻想成为劳工阶层一员就是个例子。在其他时候，幻想是对人物不完整的经历所作的补充，探索了他们在不同的环境下可能成为的样子，比如在以新西兰为背景的作品中，琳达和贝莉尔梦想着能够改变自己，便是很好的例子。曼斯菲尔德最成功的一些作品中创造了一个实际上是由幻想和模拟的现实相结合的世界。现实场景揭示了事实的真相，而幻想场景则揭示了情感的真相。通过二者的互动，读者可以获得对客观现实和主观现实的共同认知。

幻想作为一种特殊的虚构技巧也加强了曼斯菲尔德叙事的现实深度。曼斯菲尔德通过幻想的两个基本特征，即人物对真和美的诚挚追求，以及他们对人类残酷生存状态的愤慨，充分证明了它是"严肃文学"不可分割的一个成分。

早在1918年，曼斯菲尔德就把她写作的冲动归咎于"两种驱使力"：其一是"真正的快乐"，或者说"某种极其幸福的**平静**心态"；其二是"觉得所有一切都注定要毁灭的**极为**深切的无助感"，或者说"内心想**抵抗毁坏的呐喊**"（*Letters to Murry* 149）。这两种"驱使力"解释了她笔下人物的灵魂苦役以及他们的幻想世界的本质特性。

她小说中所呈现的人际关系是复杂的，因为大部分主人公都经受了来自

"最深爱、最信任的人"的伤害（Zinman 458）。被麻木不仁的性伴侣或者专横的父母亲所虐，是曼斯菲尔德女性角色的主要痛苦来源，正如《序曲》和《在海湾》中的琳达、《画像》（"Pictures"）中的莫斯小姐和《已故上校的女儿》中的康斯坦西娅和约瑟芬所经受的那样。

但是生命的痛苦并不仅仅只是强加给女性的，曼斯菲尔德笔下描绘的一些男性角色也同样在悲哀的生活困境中挣扎，或沦为以虚荣和势利为中心的女性世界的牺牲品，比如《一个无趣的男人》中那个可怜男主人公，以及《时髦的婚姻》中那个被操控的丈夫。老年人也是受害者，他们活在已逝青春的记忆里，并努力应对年老和死亡的现实，如《布瑞尔小姐》《苍蝇》和《帕克大妈的一生》中的主角。年少无知之人也未能幸免，不得不为他们想闯入成人认知和经验世界的冲动付出沉重代价，就像《她的第一次舞会》中的莱拉和《家庭女教师》中的女主人公一样。由于曼斯菲尔德小说中的大多数人物都是软弱无能、深受困惑、孤立无助的，他们表达欲望和愤怒的唯一途径，只能是通过幻想。

曼斯菲尔德在作品中运用幻想揭示了人性的两个方面：对美好事物的自然渴望，和对丑陋事物的自然厌恶，这种厌恶也就是她所说的"抵抗毁坏的呐喊"，这两个方面在她的小说中经常是密切交织在一起的。对美和真理的渴望有时通过一种虚幻的幸福感来表现，而当这种渴望不可避免地遭遇失望甚至幻灭时，小说人物的声音就渐渐转化为愤怒和义愤。《幸福》中伯莎的困惑徘徊，可以看作是《园会》中劳拉对生活意义的热切追求的延续。贝莉尔对自我认同的急切渴望和琳达摆脱婚姻陷阱的梦想，可能会发展成布瑞尔小姐对年老和孤独的恐惧，或者帕克大妈对人类严酷生存状态的抗议呐喊。幻想反映出他们想寻找更好生活的真诚渴望，也显示了他们遍寻不得时所经历的痛苦心境。幻想的这些特征揭示了人性的深层真相，有助于确立曼斯菲尔德作为二十世纪严肃作家的文学地位。

注：中文译文部分出现的引文及参考文献索引，请参见英文原文之后所附的参考书目清单。